ASYLUM

B. LOVE

PROLIFIC PEN PUSHER

PREFACE

Mood: "Asylum" by John Legend

Asylum

L ate October

Some things you had to see to believe. Some things you never wanted to see. Two of my tenants having sex was at the top of that list. I'd been getting complaints from the tenants at my asylum on Jefferson that Michael and Unique were having sex two and three times a day.

The problem with that was they were housed in an open space for all to see. When I welcomed a tenant into the asylum, they had to agree to spend their time working, going to school, or attending therapy sessions depending on why they were temporarily in my care. If they didn't take their agreement seriously or handled their responsibilities quickly, I could understand them getting bored easily. Being bored was no excuse to have sex on a bunk bed for ten other people to see.

They were so deep in what they were doing, they didn't even hear me come in. The closer I got, the worse the smell

1

became. I wasn't sure if they'd come in and got to business after working or what, but they had the space funky as hell. Since they wanted to act like animals, I decided to treat them like animals.

I wrapped my hand around Michael's neck and lifted him off Unique's body.

"Agh!" he yelled as I tossed him onto the floor.

"Didn't I tell y'all not to be having sex in here?" I confirmed, looking from one to the other.

The six tenants that were at the round dinner table playing cards began to laugh and whisper among themselves as Unique quickly shuffled to cover herself with the thin blanket on the bottom bunk bed. I didn't know why she was acting shameful now. She was just moaning with her legs spread wide for this nigga.

"Asylum," Michael called, trying to step in my direction.

Lifting my hand, I turned slightly to avoid the sight of his naked frame. "Put some clothes on, man. Don't nobody wanna see that shit."

As irritated as I was, the laughter coming from the dining area lightened my mood. I was all for freedom and being comfortable in one's sexuality, but this was too much. They scrambled for their clothing while I headed into the kitchen. Dan was standing by the refrigerator. He opened it, and I grabbed a bottle of water to sip on while I waited for them to get dressed.

My eyes scanned the area, and pride filled me over what I'd created. The one level space was two thousand square feet. It had enough beds to sleep twelve and an area for four cribs in case any of my tenants had babies. They had a living room, dining area, kitchen, and gaming area for adults and kids. The only area that was closed off to provide privacy were the bathrooms. I had six walk-in showers, sinks, and three garden tubs for each gender.

Creating asylums all over Memphis wasn't my original plan, but after a brief stint working for the Memphis Police Department, this seemed like a better fit for me. I offered a haven for people from all walks of life. Some came to my asylums through witness protection or police custody, which allowed me to receive government grants. Others came through referrals and recommendations. Regardless, I never turned anyone away.

The only time a person was forced to leave before their contract expired was if they disrespected me or someone on my team or broke the rules. Unique was hiding from an abusive ex whose gang was actively searching for her, and Michael was waiting for a murderer's trial to be completed before he returned to his normal life. Several threats had been made against Michael, and that was the only reason I would allow him to stay in my program.

When they were presentable, I had them meet me outside so we could talk. The amount of space between them wouldn't have suggested they were just fucking like they'd been together for years. Crazy part was, Unique hadn't been here for more than three days.

"Why my tenants been sending word through the team that y'all around here fucking like rabbits?" Michael opened his mouth to speak, and I could tell he was about to say some bullshit. "And before you lie, I literally just caught y'all, so please don't waste my time."

While he released a frustrated huff, Unique stepped toward me. She grabbed my hand and looked up at me with pleading eyes. "I'm sorry, Asylum. Whatever you want me to do, I'll do. Just please... don't put me out."

"I'm going to separate y'all. And since y'all seem to have

too much free time on your hands, I'm putting you both on cooking and kitchen duties at your new locations."

Relief covered both of their faces as I pulled my hand from Unique's. Being here, you were bound to connect with someone unless you were intentionally closed off to it. I urged them to have a family mentality, and one of the ways I did that was making sure they cooked and had dinner together. They were allowed to volunteer for other duties such as cleaning, but when people needed more structure, I selected jobs for them.

"Thank you so much, Asylum," Unique said.

"I really appreciate this," Michael added.

"Just follow the rules," I tossed over my shoulder as I walked away.

I couldn't help but chuckle as Merc grinned at the sight of me. He was probably my closest confidant and the head of security. While he was never stationed at one asylum for too long, he bounced from one to another throughout the day. If I trusted anyone with my life, it would be Merc. Between him and my best friend Haley, I kept my circle small.

"Mannn, say," he dragged as we shook hands. "They really in there getting busy?"

"Like they getting paid for it." We laughed. "Lights on, room full of people, and they goin' at it."

"Damn. I guess they gotta get it how they live."

"Not in here."

"Where you puttin' 'em?"

I thought it over for a while before saying, "Have Bully take Unique to the asylum in Lakeland and Michael can go to the one in the east."

"Aight, bet."

We shook hands again before I headed to my truck. Out

of my two cars, the RAM 1500 was the one I drove throughout the day. I usually pulled my Challenger out at night and on weekends.

After getting into my truck, I grabbed my phone from the cupholder to check my notifications. True had called me twice, which was unusual. Usually, my girl didn't call me unless she wanted something before I got back home. We had a routine in place, and she knew if I wasn't there when she got out of school that I was working, so she didn't bother me. The fact that she had called twice was a bit unsettling.

I called her back and maneuvered my way through the wooded area filled with trees that allowed my asylum to remain hidden. The only way a person could find it was if they were brought to it.

It took a few rings, but True eventually answered with, "Hey, Daddy Sy."

Every time I heard her say that, it made me smile. I hated when people called True my stepdaughter. Having my DNA wouldn't have made her more my child than she already was. The twelve-year-old princess had embedded her way into my heart the moment I knew there was a chance she was mine. When her mother and I had the DNA test done and we learned she shared the DNA of another man, it broke my heart. But holding her in my arms after Sierra gave birth restored me. True had been my girl ever since.

"Hey, baby girl. You good?"

True sighed into the phone. She was hesitating, and I wasn't sure why. "I'm OK."

"What is it, True?"

"Mama isn't here, and I was wondering if you could

have me something delivered on Uber Eats. I tried to do it, but I don't have any more money in my account."

My grip on the steering wheel instantly tightened. I hated how independent Sierra wanted True to be. To me, she was too young to be worrying about ordering food for herself, making appointments, or even being at home by herself for long periods of time. I understood why Sierra wanted True to be able to do certain things on her own, but to me, she needed to remain a dependent child for as long as she could. Still, there were certain decisions Sierra could make without me since True wasn't my child biologically. Even with them staying with me, on some things, I had to yield.

"Did Sierra tell you where she was going?"

"No, sir. She wasn't here when I got home."

That was odd. Sierra didn't have a job and she hadn't called to tell me she had anything to do, so I was surprised to hear that she wasn't at home.

"Aight, baby girl. I'ma put three hundred dollars in the account, and you can order whatever you want. I'll cook dinner for later when I get there."

"OK. I think I want the tamales with chili and cheese. Do you want me to get enough for you?"

"Yeah, go ahead and get the twelve piece."

We talked for a few seconds more before ending the call, and as soon as we did, I called Sierra. She didn't answer, which alarmed me even more. I tried not to think the worst, but in my line of work that was hard to do. I called again and texted her, asking that she hit me up ASAP. At a red light, I checked my security cameras to see when she'd left and how her demeanor was. Because I had cameras in and outside of my home, I had the notifications off most of the time.

My concern grew more when I saw that Sierra had temporarily cut the cameras off.

What the fuck was she doing that she didn't want me to see?

It was nearing nine p.m., and I still hadn't seen or heard from Sierra. The moment I made it home, True became my priority and I cut my work phone off. Regardless of the connections and government contracts I had, nothing came before True—not even her mama. I spent a few hours making sure she was good. We did her homework and studied for a vocabulary test she had in the morning. After that, we watched a movie, and I made her favorite fried chicken wings with honey and pepperoncini peppers. I'd gotten her hooked on eating it like that, now she wanted it once or twice a week.

True had retired to her bedroom after taking a shower and reading a chapter in her bible. Since eight, she'd been free to do whatever she wanted until her ten o'clock bedtime. I didn't want to alarm her about Sierra, but I'd been calling and texting her nonstop. At first, my calls were going through, and she just wasn't answering. Now, it was as if the phone had been cut off altogether. There was no point in me reaching out to the police until after twenty-four hours had passed, but I did check hospitals and the intake database to make sure she wasn't sick or hadn't been arrested for anything.

I checked the room and quite a few of her clothes were missing. My ego didn't want to accept the fact that she'd left me. My heart wouldn't allow me to accept the fact that she'd left her child. None of it made sense. I went out to her she-shed, and that was where she had a letter, signed divorce papers, and her wedding ring waiting for me. It shouldn't have surprised me that she left it in here, because she knew I hated coming out here. This, to her, would be the last place I came—giving her a good head start to wherever she was going.

After making my way to the egg-shaped chair in the center of the room, I plopped down and tried to steel myself for what I was about to read.

ASYLUM,

I'M SORRY. I had to leave. It was too much for me. I know you could find me if you really wanted to, so I'm asking that you let me go. I've tossed my phone so you can't track me and I'm not taking the car. Tell True I love her, and I had to do what was best for me, which is going to be what's best for her. Sign those divorce papers. You didn't want to be with me anymore anyway, right? I don't know when I'll come back, if ever, but when I do... you'll be free to be with someone else.

I love you... maybe too much.
SiSi

ALL I COULD DO WAS chuckle as I read the letter over again. Sierra and I had known each other for thirteen years. A one-night stand tied me to her for what I thought would be for life. Even after finding out True wasn't mine, I stayed. Sierra had gone through a lot to get me, and even with the problems we'd been having lately, it didn't make sense for her to leave.

Was she trying to make me miss her?

Was she trying to teach me a lesson?

I wasn't sure.

The only thing I was sure of was that this little disappearing act of hers wouldn't just drive a wedge between us; but it would break her daughter's heart too.

After leaving her she-shed, I went back inside and contemplated what I wanted to tell True, if I told her anything at all. I hoped this was just a stupid game Sierra was playing and that she'd be back in the morning. If not, I didn't know what the hell I was going to do.

M y divorce was officially finalized, and for the first time in a year, I felt like I could finally breathe. Trey insisted on months of mediation, and the only thing that made him finally sign those papers was my lawyer threatening to add his new baby by another woman to the record—which would not only force him to pay me alimony but also go against the morality clause his family business had. Trey's family was all about their reputation, and that was why all of Trey Clark's dark and dirty deeds were done privately. I was just grateful he agreed to the divorce to avoid them coming to the light.

I had no desire to remain tied to Trey in any way, and that was why I declined monthly alimony. My sister, Dallas, swore I was a damn fool for turning the money down. Instead, we agreed to Trey removing himself as co-partner of my staffing agency. To me, having one hundred percent ownership of my company and freedom from him was worth more. He requested to see me once the decree was filed, and I agreed to speed up the process of him signing.

So my parents accompanied me to my attorney's office, where Trey was supposed to meet me with his.

As I sat at the conference table and waited for him to arrive, I couldn't help but think back on how I'd gotten to this point in my life. When I met Trey, he was perfect. Not the kind of perfect where he said and did the right things suspiciously, but the kind of perfect where we vibed and put forth effort that made me trust we'd have forever together. Forever turned into five years married after a year of dating, and though that was disappointing, I'd rather get over that feeling than remain in a toxic marriage that drained me of my peace and happiness.

The sound of the door creaking caused me to turn slightly and look. Trey looked good, as always. He favored the actor Michael Bolwaire... body and all. His wide, stocky build was one of the things I loved about Trey. It always made me feel safe with him. Now, I felt the opposite. I didn't feel safe with the man who valued me enough to give me his last name in marriage, a holy and sacred union, and that was probably the most heartbreaking part of all of this.

Confusion covered Trey's face as he took slow steps into the room.

"You couldn't come alone?"

My head shook. "I didn't know what you were up to, so I asked my parents to come just to be safe."

With a chuckle and shake of his head, Trey made his way over to me. "You scared of me now?" Between his wide stance and crooked grin, I wasn't sure how serious of a question that was.

"Whatever you want to talk to her about, you can do so in front of us," my father, Hamilton, said.

Toward the end of our marriage, Trey and I did a lot of arguing. He'd pushed me and grabbed me, but he had never smacked or punched me. Mama said that was more than enough. One night, our argument was so heated he choked and dangled me over the balcony, threatening to drop me if I even *considered* leaving him. That was my breaking point. I went home to my parents, and after my father saw the handprint around my neck, he grabbed his pistol and took me right back home—where he expected me to beat the shit out of Trey while he had a gun pointed at him to make sure he never thought about putting his hands on me again.

As angry and hurt as I was, I'd always loved Trey too much to want to do anything to intentionally hurt him. All I did was pack my bags knowing Daddy would keep me safe. What was even crazier was the fact that, the following weekend, Trey found out he had gotten the woman he cheated on me with pregnant. He hadn't planned for me to find out about her, but she showed up at the house demanding he stopped ignoring her. I watched the whole thing play out on the security camera while the rest of our neighbors got a front row seat to his ratchet ass drama.

By that point, I had already made up my mind to divorce him, but that caused me to expedite the process. I wasn't sure what made my husband cheat on me. I gave him literally any and everything he wanted and needed. Oftentimes over the past year, I wondered if I was too good of a woman. Maybe I loved him too easily and he wanted someone who presented a challenge. Either way, I was glad to finally be divorced from Trey, and I hoped today would be the last day I ever had to lay eyes on him.

"I'm not here to cause my wife..."

"Ex-wife," my mother, Drew, corrected.

Trey gritted his teeth. "I'm not here to cause Dauterive any trouble or pain. I was hoping we could have one last chance to talk. That's it."

I knew Trey wouldn't let up, so I obliged. Standing, I assured my parents that I would be OK as I followed Trey outside the conference room. Because of the wide windows, they would be able to see us. Crossing my arms over my chest, I shifted my weight to one side as I waited for him to speak. Whatever he had to say must have been important. Since we were once business partners as well, I didn't want to risk not hearing him out because we were no longer married.

"Thank you," he mumbled.

"Just say what you have to say, Trey, please."

With one bob of his head, Trey shoved his hands into his tan slacks. "I'm sorry, love. For all this shit." I was sure there was more he had to say, so I remained silent. "We were having our issues, and I shouldn't have stepped out on you. I never meant to have a baby on you."

"You know how I felt about cheating, Trey, but that wasn't why I divorced you. You getting someone else pregnant was confirmation that I had made the right decision to divorce you."

He looked at me as if I was speaking a different language. Scoffing, he crossed his arms over his chest and closed the space between us.

"What could I have possibly done to make you divorce me, Dauterive?"

"I'm sorry, were you not paying attention during mediation? Things had gotten toxic as hell between us. You're a narcissistic manipulator who wanted to control me." His eyes rolled and tongue rolled over his cheek as I continued. "I allowed you to damn near brainwash me with an obsessive love that neither of us was capable of keeping up with. The more I tried to get from under your thumb the crazier you started to act. And let's not forget when you would get physical. On top of all of that, you had the nerve to go and start a relationship with another woman while we were separated, knowing what happened the last time a man did that to me. And you're going to stand here and expect me to believe you think the only reason we're over is the baby? You did the one thing I told you not to do."

"Doe, I'm sorry." He gently grabbed my hands, but I pulled them away. Sighing, he put some space between us. "I was hoping we could start over. Things were good between us before we got married. I think that piece of paper put a lot of pressure on the both of us. But if we got back to dating…"

A bark of laughter escaped me as I lifted my hands. "No."

"No?" he repeated loudly, causing Daddy to stand. "The fuck you mean no?"

"I mean exactly what I said. I divorced you because I want nothing to do with you. What part of that do you not understand?"

"The part where you think it's going to be that easy for you to get away from me." His teeth gritted as he added, "You're mine, Doe. I ain't letting up off you for nothing in this world."

"I think it's time for you to leave, Trey," Daddy said, making his way next to us.

Trey's jaw clenched as he stared at me. "This isn't over, Dauterive."

"Actually, it is," Mama said, grabbing my hand.

I didn't realize I was holding my breath until he walked away and I released it. Swallowing hard, I pulled in a deep breath. I didn't want to show how much the exchange had gotten to me, so I gave Mama a forced smile as she stroked my hand with her thumb.

"I want you to stay with us," she said. "Something about that boy is unhinged."

"I agree," Daddy said. "I was surprised he finally signed the papers, but it's clear he's not done with this yet."

"Whether he is or he isn't, I am. I'm not going to live my life in fear. I just found the home I want to spend a few years in, and I'm not going to let Trey rob me of that."

I could tell by their expressions that they didn't agree with me, but they didn't push it. After thanking them both for coming, I led them outside. My best friend, Nicole, wanted to throw me a divorce party but I declined. I didn't want to celebrate the failure of my marriage even though it was a new beginning that returned me to my freedom. Instead, I planned to spend the evening on a solo date. All I could do was pray Trey lost interest in me eventually... especially since he had a newborn baby to take care of.

Asylum

E arly November

A WEEK HAD PASSED, and Sierra had yet to return. Her phone service was disconnected. I had a tracker on her car for emergencies, and it led me to a car lot where she traded it in for a hooptie that I couldn't track. Since it was clear she was driving and using cash, I was unable to find her... which was exactly what she wanted.

Even with the problems we were having, I didn't expect her to do something this extreme. She hadn't just abandoned me; she'd abandoned her daughter too. Regardless of how I felt, I could logically navigate my feelings. True was a twelve-year-old girl. She hadn't mastered emotional intelligence yet.

I hadn't been able to tell her the truth about Sierra. So far, I had shared that Sierra needed a vacation, and where she went, her mother wasn't allowed to use her phone. I didn't know how long that lie would stick because she'd admitted to missing her and wanting desperately to talk to her. True asked me to call the hotel where her mother was staying so she could talk to her, and I told her I didn't know how to get in touch with her. She told me I could find anyone and do anything, and that shit almost broke me to my core.

Since True was born, I took great pride in giving baby girl whatever she wanted. But this was one thing I felt like I'd failed her with. If only I had let shit ride with Sierra, she'd still be here, and I wouldn't have to witness True's heart breaking piece by piece every day.

When I felt completely empty but too proud to go to my grandparents and tell them what was going on, I went to Haley. She'd been gone for a week with Antonne, and I hated to put my burden on her, but I needed my best friend. As soon as they pulled up, she was making her way over to me.

"Tell me what's wrong so I can fix it," she pleaded, lowering my hands from my face to look into my eyes. I'd gotten lost in my thoughts as I sat on her front porch awaiting her arrival.

"It's Sierra." My head shook as I struggled to find the words. "She's gone."

"Gone?" Haley repeated. "What do you mean gone?"

I chuckled and ran my tongue over my cheek before swallowing hard. "I mean she left. She left me a note, talking about don't try to find her, divorce papers she'd already signed along with her ring, and she left."

"What about True? Did she take True with her?"

I shook my head again. "No, and she has to know I'm not letting her deadbeat ass daddy get her back. Now I gotta deal with his bullshit on top of hers."

"OK, something isn't right. There's no way Sierra would

just leave you and leave True behind. When did this happen? Have you called the police? Are you trying to find her?"

I wished it was something more serious. That maybe someone had kidnapped her and was using her for ransom... or to blackmail me. That would have been easier for my ego to digest. But that wasn't the case. She'd left us, and from the looks of it, Sierra really had no plans of coming back.

"You good, brotha?" Antonne asked as he made his way toward us.

"I will be," I grumbled, squeezing Haley's hands gently as I looked into her eyes.

"Good. I gotta go, bae," Antonne told her. "Doe has been blowing my phone up and the last text said if anything happened to her it was because of her ex-husband. She's never done some shit like this."

Upon hearing his words, I stood. "You need me to go with you?"

Antonne's head shook. "Not if yo' head won't be in it."

"My head is always in it when it comes to this."

"Aight, let's go."

"Y'all be careful," Haley said as we headed to Antonne's Bronco. "And make sure you bring him back so I can make sure he's good, Stink."

The first part of the ride was silent... like Antonne held it in until he couldn't hold it in anymore. He lowered the Yo Gotti that was playing and asked, "You wanna talk about it?"

Even though my head shook, I shared, "She left."

A few seconds of silence passed. "I'm not trying to be funny, but I didn't think you would care if she did."

That made me smile for the first time today because it

was true. I always treated Sierra with love and respect publicly and privately. When things started to shift between us after we celebrated our last anniversary, I shared with Haley and Antonne what happened. I also told them I didn't want to be married to her anymore. Sierra knew I was sticking around for True.

Because of how I was brought up, I wanted her to have a two-parent household until she left for college. I wanted to make sure that when she became an adult, she knew she could always count on me, regardless of things ending between me and her mother. At first, Sierra said she was cool with that because she believed there was still a chance of things going back to normal between us, but apparently, she changed her mind.

"Honestly, if SiSi would have come to me and said I was right about us getting a divorce, we could have split amicably. I would have supported her and still been there for True. But she chose to run away, and that shit has been fucking with me for the past week."

"Does True know?"

"Nah. I couldn't stomach telling her that her mother abandoned her, just like my mother had abandoned me. I know that pain all too well. Plus, I was hoping Sierra would have returned by now."

"Have you tried looking for her?"

"Yeah. She has to be using cash wherever she is, because I have alerts on all the cards. She switched cars and cut off her phone."

"Damn! She really ain't tryna be found."

"Man, say. And if it wasn't for True, I'd let her ass stay a ghost."

"Sorry to hear that, bro. For you and True. She's good with you, though. Ain't no doubt about that."

I nodded and expressed my thanks for his faith before the conversation shifted. I asked him, "You said something is going on with somebody's husband?"

"Yeah... Doe." He scratched his head, continuing to talk, but his words were going in one ear and out of the other. *Doe.* I used to be in love with a woman named Dauterive, and we called her Doe. Quite frankly, I was still in love with her now. There was no reason for me to think it was the same one, but just the mention of that name put her right in the forefront of my mind. "She's in an abusive marriage or some shit?"

"To be honest, I don't know what's goin' on with her. I told her she could come to me when she was ready to talk a while ago and she said OK, but this is the first time she's reached out about him. Their divorce was finalized a week or so ago, so he's probably showing his ass. Doe is the kind of woman that if you lose her... it's truly a loss."

"Is that her real name?"

"It's Dauterive."

"Jersey?"

"Yeah." He looked over at me briefly. "You know her?"

My heart instantly began to palpitate. It was one thing knowing Doe was in trouble, but knowing she was having issues with her ex took my anxiety to a different level. I had prepared to be the man she spent the rest of her life with. She was supposed to be my wife instead of Sierra. Hearing that she was possibly in an abusive relationship had me ready to blow the world up behind her.

"Very well." Antonne had been around for the last five years, so I understood why he was unaware of my past with Doe. She was the best part of my past... my life... outside of True. "We were engaged."

He chuckled, smacking my chest with the back of his

hand. "Hol' up. You the nigga I've had to hear stories about over the years?"

"Stories?" I sat up in my seat. "What kind of stories?"

Antonne's head shook as he licked the corner of his mouth. "I'on know if it's my place to share that. Doe is one of my oldest friends and we *just* reconnected. A lot of shit she shared was in confidence." I could respect that. "What I will say is... my friend truly loved you."

Even if I wanted to deny it, I couldn't stop, "God knows I loved her too," from slipping out of my lips.

Silence found us again, and I was cool with that. Dauterive was in trouble. I was about to see my Doe. My mind was racing a mile a minute. All I could think about was the time we spent together.

We dated all throughout college and planned to get married. After getting heavy in our careers, we lost our commitment to each other. Doe and I were friends above all, so we never had real issues. Even when we had disagreements, we handled that shit with respect and love. It was crazy, but we took notes when we were upset with each other to make sure we didn't have the same hurt feelings and problems repeatedly. I didn't think anything would separate us, but a heated argument, brief breakup, and one night stand had done just that.

I didn't realize how deep I'd gotten into my thoughts until we were pulling into a driveway.

"Is that fire?" Antonne asked.

I searched the front of the house, eyes locking on a blaze from a room upstairs.

"Shit!" Hopping out quickly, I rushed toward the front door, and Antonne wasn't too far behind. After getting the door kicked down, I charged up the stairs while Antonne called for help. "Doe!" I yelled, getting no answer back. I was sure she was in the room where the fire had started.

Antonne was searching for the fire extinguisher in the laundry room since it wasn't in the kitchen. After grabbing the comforter from the only bedroom upstairs that the fire hadn't rapidly spread to, I went into the bathroom and soaked it in the shower. By the time I was done, the fire had reached the hallway.

I covered myself with the wet comforter and held my breath. The knob was so hot smoke lifted as I opened it with the comforter. There was so much smoke and fire I could barely see. The only thing keeping me from feeling the flames and coughing like crazy was the comforter, and I was grateful for that.

Doe was behind the door. She was half dressed, and I could only assume she was asleep when the fire started. Her mattress was over her, shielding her from the flames, but she was unresponsive. I picked her up and carried her out of the room with the comforter around us both. I didn't know what the fuck had happened here, but I knew if she didn't wake up soon, whoever was responsible would be buried soon after her.

Dauterive

The voices around me had dulled. All I could do was stare at the muted TV. If I paid attention to what they were saying, I would probably cry.

The last thing I remembered was going to have a glass of wine before heading home for the day. One glass of wine had me feeling very weird. I was extremely tired, to the point where I barely made it out of my clothes before I was crashing in bed.

I thought I was dreaming, but I vaguely remembered hearing Trey's voice and seeing his face. He said he was going to make sure I had no choice *but* to come back to him. After that, I was knocked out until I woke up hot and coughing uncontrollably. The next thing I remember was trying to find my phone, which I couldn't, then using a mattress to shield myself from flames. I didn't know how long the fire had been raging before I woke up and how much smoke I had inhaled, but by the time I made it to the door, I was passing out.

Now, I was in the hospital with IVs and oxygen trying

not to break into sobs. The doctor had come in and explained I was low on oxygen which put a strain on my heart. It had stopped, but thankfully, Antonne had gotten me to the hospital before it was too late. He was sitting in the corner dozing off while my parents and sister talked to the doctor. He wanted to keep me until my oxygen returned to normal, which I understood and appreciated.

Thankfully, I didn't have any severe burns. By the time Antonne had gotten to me, the mattress hadn't burned through yet. That had to be God telling me to get the mattress because with the way I was feeling, I didn't see how I was in my right mind.

"Ant," I called. My voice was hoarse, and my throat was sore. After coughing, Mama gave me a cup of water while Antonne made his way over to me. I took his hand into mine and kissed it. "You saved my life."

He gave me a soft smile and shook his head. "It wasn't me. I'm glad I took my phone off airplane mode when I did, but it wasn't me that carried you out that room."

"Then who was it?"

"Asylum."

My heart monitor began to race, gaining everyone's attention. There weren't too many men walking around the city with that name. In fact, I only knew of one.

"Asylum?" I repeated quietly. "Matthews?"

"Yeah. He tried to stay up here until you woke up, but he had to get back home to True."

True.

Was that his son... or his daughter?

Sierra was his wife.

I'd learned that devastating truth in the worst way twelve years ago.

"Oh. Well..." My head shook as confusion filled me. I wasn't sure what they were doing together, but I was grateful to God for Asylum. Without them, there was no doubt in my mind that I'd be dead. "T-tell him I said thanks."

Chuckling, Antonne lowered himself and gave me a kiss on the temple. "You can tell him yourself. He'll be up here tomorrow."

"Bu—I... Antonne..."

"Call me if you need me. I'll come up here and check on you in the morning."

"We—wait!" Trying to yell after him was not a good idea. I had another coughing spell, which caused the doctor to let us know he'd be bringing me some medicated cough drops I could suck to help soothe my throat and help with the swelling of my airways.

"Asylum..."

Asylum had always been just that: a safe space and the man whose love drove me crazy.

"Shh, rest, baby. We can talk a little later. You need to rest," Mama insisted.

As much as I wanted to get to the bottom of what the hell had happened, she was right. Just that brief interaction had taken a lot out of me. Before I knew it, I was falling back asleep.

I was ready for these detectives to leave. I knew they were just doing their job, but the questions were frustrating me. They had me run down my entire day. I felt like they didn't believe me. Even though I only had one drink, they accused me of being drunk and not remembering what transpired when I made it home. Apparently, I left my phone and purse in my car before going inside.

"Even if she was drunk, which she wasn't, that ain't got shit to do with the arson that started in her room," Daddy said. "Y'all don't have no information about that? No explanation as to why a fire was started in her bedroom of all places?"

"No, sir. We're not firefighters," the youngest one said.

When my mother's head jerked back and she laughed, I knew it was in their best interest to get the hell up out my room. My parents didn't play when it came to their daughters. They would go against *anyone* to protect us.

"We know that, smart ass," Dallas said, gently pulling Mama behind her.

"Why in the hell are y'all here?" Daddy asked. "Other than to accuse my daughter of something that isn't true."

"We're trying to find the person responsible for this. The fire department has confirmed the fire was started intentionally," the second, older one said. He was Black, and I could tell he spent a lot of his shift being a buffer between the community and his young, white partner. "It was a slow starter. They don't think it was meant to cause serious damage, but because you were asleep for as long as you were, it had more time to spread. Can you think of anyone you encountered today or at all that could have possibly followed you to harm you?"

I thought about it briefly before shaking my head. "No, but can't you go to the bar I went to just to make sure no one drugged and followed me? Maybe check some cameras? I'm a hundred percent sure someone had to at least slip a sleeping pill in my drink. There was no reason for me to be as tired and out of it as I was when I got home. I'm not so

26

heavy of a sleeper that I wouldn't have heard someone in my ro—"

My mind thought back to the dream I thought I'd had about Trey. Refusing to believe he could have had a hand in this, I didn't want to admit what I remembered. There was no chance Trey could have had me drugged. And even if he did, could he try to kill me by setting my home on fire?

"What is it, baby?" Daddy asked. "Are you remembering something?"

Nibbling my bottom lip, I fought against my loyalty to Trey. "I thought this was a dream. I'm sure it was a dream."

"What is it?" the second officer asked. I looked at his nametag as he stepped closer to the hospital bed, tightening his grip on his small, black notepad.

"I thought I dreamed about my ex-husband. He was hovering over me while I was in bed."

"Today?" Officer Stanley asked. I nodded. "Did he say anything?"

My eyes shifted toward my family before my head hung. Sniffling, I shrugged and shook my head.

"It's hazy, but I think he said he was going to make sure I had no choice but to come back to him."

"That son of a bitch!" Daddy roared.

"But I, I really don't think he did this," I added quickly. "Trey is a lot of things, but he's not a murderer. I don't think he would try to kill me."

"Are you crazy, sis? That man is capable of just about anything now that you've left him. It might not have been his plan to kill you, but from the sound of it, he for damn sure wanted to make you dependent on him again. I wouldn't be surprised if he was somewhere watching your house burn!"

"Look..." Lifting my hands, I took a deep breath. "Unless

there's evidence to prove he had something put in my drink, followed me home, and set my house on fire... I don't want to put this on him."

"We'll get his information and have a conversation with him," Stanley said.

I was OK with that. I didn't want my loyalty to make me a fool. If Trey was responsible for this, he deserved to pay. I also didn't want paranoia to have me blaming an innocent man. Trey wanted me back, but I couldn't accept him going to extremes such as this to make that happen.

Asylum

I could no longer hide the truth from True. She'd gone to her grandmother, Selena, and told her Sierra and I were hiding something from her. True was very worried, and I hated she was in this position. At this point, I decided it was better to tell her the truth than to have her mind swirling around with a million questions.

We were on the way to her grandparents' house. I wanted to check in on Doe and I didn't want to leave True home alone. Plus, because of how much she was missing Sierra, I figured it would do her some good to spend some time with the people that were the closest thing to her mom outside of herself.

"We need to talk," I told her after cutting the radio down.

"Are you finally going to tell me about what's going on with my mom?"

She shifted in her seat slightly to face me, but I kept my eyes on the road. Squeezing the back of my neck, I nodded.

"Yeah, baby girl. I am."

29

"OK. So where is she?"

"I don't know."

"You don't know?"

"No. She didn't tell me where she was going."

"How could she leave and not tell you where she was going?"

"She didn't want me to be able to find her."

True was silent for a while. "She ran away?"

"Yeah, in a way... she did."

"Why? Did I do something wrong?"

The innocence of her question and her voice made my heart squeeze. Taking her hand into mine, I shook my head.

"Not at all, True. It had *nothing* to do with you. Your mom had some things she needed to work out, and she thought it would be best if she did it alone."

"But why can't we talk to her? She doesn't want to talk to me anymore?"

Gritting my teeth, I thought over my words carefully. I hated Sierra for putting us in this situation. Even if she wanted to say to hell with me, she should have talked to True before she left... or took her with her. It would have broken my heart, but every daughter needed her mother. I was doing everything I could for True, however, I'd never be able to take Sierra's place in her life. I still hadn't figured out her end game. What was the reason for her leaving True behind?

"No, baby. She does. Mama just needed to detach from life for a bit." I paused and tried to think of a way to explain this that would make the most sense and keep her from taking it personally. "You remember when you tried out for the track team last year?"

"Yes, sir."

"And you remember when you got so overwhelmed with that and school that you decided to take a break?"

"Mhm."

"Well... your mom needed a break from her life. Not you personally, just life itself. She needed to take some time to rest and get her mind and heart together. But it wasn't because she didn't want you or to talk to you. She loves you, and she can't wait to get back home to you."

I was worried she wouldn't believe me, but that seemed to satisfy her because she gave me a soft, "OK." With a huff, she looked out the window as she tightened her grip on my hand. "Hopefully she will get enough rest soon. I'm ready for her to come back home. Even though I'm mad at her for leaving me, I miss her."

I hated to admit it, but I couldn't help but say, "Me too."

I WAS nervous as I entered Dauterive's room, but the moment I laid eyes on her, that anxiety left me. It didn't matter how much time had passed between us, being in her presence today felt just like it did thirteen years ago. To keep myself from kissing her, I stayed at the doorway. She was too busy looking at her phone, which gave me a chance to take her beauty in. Even with her having tubes in her nose and IVs in her arm, Doe was still the most beautiful woman I'd ever seen.

"Damn." Her head lifted, and at the sight of me, she whimpered. She tried to sit over the side of the bed, but I stopped her with, "Stay your ass right there and let me come to you."

Doe's arms extended, and the sight of her fingers opening and closing as she beckoned me to her made my heart light. Because of how we ended, I didn't think she'd ever be happy to see me again.

"Come here," she requested with a shaky voice that was thick with emotion.

I made my way over to her and gave her a hug that made me feel like I hadn't been embraced since the last time I had her in my arms.

I didn't want to let her go.

"I missed you," I confessed, with enough tenderness in my tone to make it shake.

She held me tighter and ran her hand against the back of my neck. "I missed you too," she almost whispered. "Thank you for saving my life."

"That was God. He just used me to get you out that room." Releasing her, I stared into her eyes and pushed her hair behind her ears so I could see more of her face. "How you feelin'?"

"Better now." We mirrored each other's smiles. "When Ant told me it was you, I..." Her head shook as she stumbled over her words. "This is crazy."

Her eyes scanned me fully, settling on the tattoo of her face on my neck. Doe's head tilted and eyes watered. A trembling hand lifted to caress the daily reminder I had of her. The daily reminder that made my wife feel insecurity over filling a place in my life that she'd *never* be able to fill in my heart.

"That's me?" she confirmed softly.

"Yeah."

"Sy..." She pulled me back down to her, kissing the tattoo before giving me another hug. That shit made my dick hard as fuck. Much too much time had passed since I'd felt her lips on me.

I hadn't signed and filed the divorce papers because I

was sure Sierra would be back by now. And now, I regretted not signing so I could kiss Dauterive the way I wanted to. What was I saying?

Dauterive wasn't the one that got away. She was the one who taught me how to love a woman and honor her worth. I promised myself if I ever had the chance to be with her again, nothing would stop me... not even having a wife.

Cupping her cheeks, I allowed my lips to descend toward hers. Before they could connect, the sound of someone clearing their throat behind us gained my attention.

"Well, well, who do we have here?"

A grin lifted the corners of my mouth when my eyes locked on Drew. This woman molded her daughters in her exact image. She gave them her medium height, caramel brown skin, and slanted, honey brown eyes.

"There's my ol' lady."

She was just like her child, spreading her arms for an embrace as she swooned. "Come here and give me a hug, boy. Lawd, I feel like I haven't seen you in decades!"

"How you been, Mama?"

"Good, good... grateful to you and God for saving my baby's life. If you and Antonne hadn't been there and I lost her..."

"We were and you didn't, so there's no point in even thinking about that." As we released each other, I asked her, "Where's Pops?"

"He's checking on a couple of patients since we're here, and he's going to hate that he missed you. Can you stay for a while?"

I had planned to, but I wanted to get back to True. She was cool when I first left her with her grandparents, but the more she thought about what I said the more frustrated she got over what Sierra did. It was a truly selfish act, one that couldn't be done when you had a child to consider, but Sierra did it anyway. I wanted to get back to True just to make sure she was straight.

"I can't, but I'll be back. Tell him to give me a call. My number is still the same."

At that admission, I looked back at Dauterive. I promised her I'd always keep my number the same in case she needed me. It fucked with me a little that she called Antonne when she was in trouble instead of me, but that was my ego. I was grateful she had someone she could trust with her life and safety that wasn't me. Besides, she'd probably deleted my number when she deleted me from her life.

"Alright, baby. You come back and see us, okay?"

"Yes, ma'am," I agreed before giving her another hug. When she kissed my cheek, I heard Doe suck her teeth and that made me smile. "I'll see you later, aight?"

"Promise?" she asked sweetly, making my heart skip a beat.

"You won't be able to keep me away, Doe. I promise."

After she nodded her agreement, I headed out. I hated what happened and I wanted to talk to her about it, but I was glad God had brought her back into my life.

Dauterive

We'd finished putting what was able to be salvaged from my rental property in storage and it broke my heart. I was so happy about being back on my own, and now, my home was gone. I considered staying at a hotel for a few nights, but my parents wanted me close, so I agreed to staying with them. Though I had the money and credit to move into something new immediately, mentally and emotionally, I was exhausted.

Detective Stanley had been keeping in touch. He had reached out to Trey, who denied any involvement. He'd also gone to the bar, and ironically, their security cameras didn't work. That was all Stanley planned to do. Antonne and Asylum had gone to my neighbors to see if any of them had cameras to see who had come to my home. They did, but only two stored their footage. We couldn't see who it was, and I hated to admit it, but his tall, wide frame looked exactly like Trey. With that evidence, we thought Stanley would have been able to bring Trey in, but without his face showing or car, he said that still wasn't enough proof.

I was frustrated by that, but I couldn't say I was surprised. With all the crime happening in Memphis, the police didn't take anything serious unless it was a murder. Even then, they only cared if it was someone famous or something they could prove.

After we had everything in storage, I treated my parents to lunch. I appreciated how dedicated they were to me and my sister. Daddy was a gynecologist who had an entire practice to run, yet he'd been making sure he was present for me. My grandma died giving birth to him, which gave my father a purpose to make sure Black women were able to have healthy deliveries and babies.

That was actually how my parents met. They both were in med school. Mama ended up working as a primary physician for five years before quitting and committing herself to being a stay-at-home wife and mom. She swore there was nothing that gave her more pride and pleasure than her family, and to me, she gave the ultimate sacrifice.

Daddy made sure he made her life easy, though. Whatever she wanted he provided, and I loved that for her.

When we made it back to their home, a piece of paper on the door caught my eye. I thought it was a delivery notice or something, so I grabbed it after going inside through the garage.

You won't get away from me.

The note was typed, but it had to be from Trey. At this point, I could no longer deny that he was behind this. I didn't think he'd stoop to such measures, but he'd been showing me that I didn't know him as well as I thought I did.

Had it not been for the fire, I would have laughed off the note. Now, I was too angry to find his antics amusing. This man had followed me home, and I was pretty sure had the bartender put something in my drink, and set my damn house on fire! All because I divorced him. Had he had this kind of dedication to being a good man and husband, he wouldn't have lost me. It seemed the less I needed him and paid him any attention the worse he acted out like a true narcissist.

After tossing the letter onto the bed I'd temporarily be sleeping in, I snatched up my phone and called him. He answered on the second ring with, "Hey, love. Ready to come home?"

"Are you ready to go to prison?"

"For what?"

"Hmm… I don't know. Maybe for having me drugged, breaking into my home, setting it on fire, and now leaving this damn note at my parents' house."

"I have no idea what you're talking about, Doe. Someone set your house on fire? You can *always* move back in with me."

There was something about the coldness of his tone that made me shiver. "Listen, Trey… You need to cut this out. You could have killed me. Is that what you really want?"

"I told you, I don't know what you're talking about. I would never do anything to hurt you, Dauterive. You know that."

Unable to stomach his lies, I ended the call. The proof of my hazy dream and the camera footage may not have been enough to convince the police that Trey was guilty, but it was for me.

"You OK in here?" Daddy asked, stepping into my room.

"No!" I didn't mean to yell at him, but I was so angry with Trey. Angry at myself for marrying Trey. "Trey left this note on the door," I said, pointing toward the note. "He's saying he didn't, but I know he did."

Daddy's expression turned into a deep frown as he read the note. "I'm going to kill him."

"Daddy, no," I begged, grabbing his arm and keeping him from leaving. "You have way too much to lose to go after Trey's crazy ass."

"I'm not going to just sit around while he harasses you."

"I'll call Detective Stanley. Maybe he can run it for prints and use it as evidence or something."

I was wrong.

Stanley had two uniformed officers come by to check things out. They said there was nothing they could do until Trey was caught in the act or physically came after me. Until then, they advised I document everything, install some cameras, and stay safe.

Daddy was pissed. I was scared he'd go back to Trey's house with his pistol without me. Lord knows I felt horrible for causing my parents this stress. I'd married the wrong man, and now, he was punishing me for finally having the courage to leave.

I WAS LOST in my thoughts on the patio when the sound of hushed voices from the inside gained my attention. The weather was beautiful this time of year, not too hot or too cold, but nothing was more beautiful than the sight of

Asylum Matthews. Seeing him at the hospital two days ago was a pleasurable blast from the past.

I used to think Asylum would have been my husband. He was the only man I'd ever truly been in love with. I loved Trey, but it wasn't the kind of love I had for Asylum. Back then, I thought that was a good thing. The love I had for Asylum hurt so much when it was over... and I never wanted to feel that again. Eventually, the hurt of our relationship ending left, and I was grateful to God for the experience to be loved by him. Some of my best memories were with Asylum. He hadn't been just my man; he was a true life partner and best friend.

Asylum and I were together during the growth stages of life. We started having trouble when we shifted from college to working adults. I could admit we didn't communicate properly and put forth the same amount of effort that we did in college. It was stressful navigating those new career paths. I didn't have my own staffing company then; I was using my HR degree. I'd landed an amazing job working for a tech company. The pay was phenomenal, but the stress was out of this world. Asylum had started on the police force, and though he loved what he did, the job weighed on his mental long after his shifts were over.

It was my belief that if we'd given each other more grace and compassion, we'd still be together now. Instead, we gave up on each other... and I'd regretted that ever since.

We stopped being partners against our problems and started having real fights. Those fights led to me breaking up with him. Me breaking up with him led to him having a one-night stand and getting *her* pregnant.

I tried to stick around and make things work, but Sierra didn't make that easy. Her whole pregnancy, while we planned the wedding, the stress made our partnership toxic, and we experienced versions of each other that didn't have the same love and respect. I decided to end the relationship before we started hating each other. Asylum asked me not to, but I couldn't stomach the idea of us becoming enemies... nor could I handle him having a baby with another woman.

What happened with Asylum was why Trey's actions hurt me so much. He knew that I'd lost the love of my life because of fighting and a brief breakup baby. For him to go out and not only cheat but do so without protection... it was like déjà vu. The biggest difference was, I had emotionally detached from Trey, so it was easier for me to let him go.

"Doe," Daddy called as he opened the back door. "Can you come inside for a moment?"

Nodding, I stood and closed my cardigan as I headed inside. I didn't want to stare at Asylum, but between the fact that so many years had passed, and he'd aged marvelously, I couldn't take my eyes off him.

He was hood nigga fine but the suit covering his tall, athletic build gave him a professional look. That suit didn't hide the tattoos on his hands and neck. The tattoo of me. I wasn't sure when he'd gotten that, but I cried after he left because of it. I wondered how Sierra felt seeing my face on her husband's body every day. I wondered why I didn't care if it hurt her. I knew she hadn't intentionally ended my relationship with Asylum, but had they not had a one-night stand that resulted in her getting pregnant, we would still be together.

Pushing those thoughts out of my head, I gave him a quick greeting before giving Daddy my attention.

"What's up?"

"I wasn't pleased with what those officers said, so I

called Antonne, and he gave me Asylum's number. I was hoping he could be of more help."

Daddy led us to the dining room, where Mama had coffee and pastries waiting. Instead of sitting across from me like Daddy had done, Asylum sat next to me. The heat of his body and scent of his cologne had chills covering my arms. I kept telling myself this was important, and I needed to focus, but I couldn't stop my eyes from going back to Sy.

Damn.

This man aged very well.

He still had the smoothest cocoa brown skin. He had a low taper on the sides of his head, but the top had hair that was braided in thick plaits that came down to his ears. His thick brows had a natural arch. And I still fell under the gaze of his hypnotic, under turned, dark eyes. When he came to the hospital, I could see his straight white teeth. Today, he had in a platinum diamond grill that looked beautiful against his round, juicy, skin-colored lips.

"Doe?" Daddy called softly.

"Hmm?"

He chuckled, looking from me to Asylum.

"I asked if you wanted to tell Sy what happened, or shall I?"

"Oh, go ahead."

I needed a little time to compose myself, and Asylum smiling at me wasn't helping—at all.

Daddy gave Asylum a rundown of what happened today. When he was done, Asylum said, "Let me guess, they aren't going to do a restraining order or question him until he does something else, or they have more concrete evidence?"

"Exactly," Daddy said. "Is there a way you can get on the case?"

"I'm not on the force anymore."

"Oh, I'm sorry. I thought you were. That's why I called."

Asylum's head shook. "Nah." He squeezed the back of his neck like he normally did when having a difficult conversation. "I quit after my partner was gunned down in front of me. By another cop no less."

"Oh no." My hand instantly covered his. "I'm sorry to hear that, Sy."

"Yeah. My partner was preparing to testify against him. The bastard had shot a Black man in broad daylight when he could have easily deescalated the situation. There were no weapons or threats. Not only did he get off for that murder, but they only gave him five years for killing my partner. Even with camera footage and my testimony."

"Wow. That's horrible. I can see why you quit."

With a sigh, Asylum shook his head. "I couldn't stay after that. I still protect and serve, though. Just in my own way."

"How so?" Daddy asked. He'd leaned further and curiosity caused his eyes to glow. They'd always had a tight bond. A bond that he'd *never* had with Trey.

"I have several asylums over the city that are used for protection. I also offer contracted security. While I do have some government contracts, the bulk of my tenants are people who find me through referrals and word on the street. I provide a safehouse for a period of time or help them get out of the city and country if needed. So I might not be on the force anymore, but I can still help."

"That's great, son," was what Daddy said.

"I'm proud of you," was what I said. "You've always been what your name means for me. I think it's fitting that you are that for others too."

He gave me a confident smile. "You used to say I drove you crazy like my name suggested, too."

We shared a soft laugh. "In a good way, though. I could never get enough of you."

My mind traveled back to a time in college when things were great between us. I was trying to study for a test, and he was sure I was overdoing it. He put together a date night for me to unwind and I declined, so he playfully kidnapped me.

"I'm gonna break up with you," I told him as he carried me out of my dorm.

"When?"

"When I've had enough of you."

"So... never?"

He swatted my ass, causing me to burst into a fit of giggles. I had an amazing time that night and woke up calm and refreshed for the test I aced.

Daddy cleared his throat, causing me to pull my eyes away from Asylum. "I'm gonna give you two some privacy to talk. Sy, let me know how much your services will be."

"For my sweetheart? I'd give my life for her. It's an honor to help, Pops. No charge at all."

Daddy shook his hand and left the room, leaving us alone. Suddenly, I was nervous.

"Thanks for helping."

"You know I'd do anything for you."

"Still?"

"Still." He pulled out an iPad. "Aight, so let's get down to business. I need to know your ex-husband's daily routine and all of the contact information you have for him. I also need his job information. Do you still have a key to the home you shared with him?"

I shook my head as I accepted the iPad and began to fill

out the form he'd pulled up. "No, I gave it back when I moved out."

"Cool. I'll get a team on this, but I'm also going to work on this personally. From the sound of it, he's reverting to a kid who isn't getting his way. The more you ignore him, don't need him, and tell him you don't want him… the more he's going to come after you."

"I can see that. Things were cool when we first got married and I allowed him to take care of me. Even when we went half on my business, things were OK as long as he had a certain level of control. When I started to take control and start spending more time alone and with my family and friends again, that's when things started to get bad between us."

"Bad how?"

I ran down the last couple of years of my marriage. The arguments, the mind games, the obsession… the cheating. As soon as I mentioned him having a baby on me, Asylum cringed.

"How's uh… your wife and baby? Well, they aren't a baby now."

Asylum gave me a smile, but it quickly faded away as his eyes shifted. "True is definitely not a baby, but she'll always be *my* baby. She's twelve going on twenty." Happiness returned to his eyes at the mention of his daughter.

"And Sierra?"

"Sierra left me… us. Me and True."

My head tilted as my brain processed his words. "She left y'all?"

His head bobbed. "Yeah. She left a note, signed divorce papers, and her ring."

I thought hearing that he wasn't still with her would make me happy in the past, but it actually pissed me off.

She was the reason, well, we were the reason we were over, but it felt better to blame her. I knew that wasn't the mature way to go about it, but I didn't care.

"Why? If I'm being too nosy just tell me to mind my business."

Asylum chuckled with a shake of his head. "Nah, I don't mind sharing. It is a long story, though."

"Well... I'm not going into the office today, so I have time." As I put what I remembered to be his favorite pastry, a cheese pastry, onto a small plate, I added, "But we really don't have to talk about this if it hurts too much."

"You remember my favorite pastry?" he confirmed.

"Of course. You were my favorite person for quite some time. You're very hard to forget... or top."

"You need to chill with that," he warned, pouring us both a cup of coffee.

"Chill with what?"

"Talking nice and making it seem like you still have feelings for me."

"I do still have feelings for you."

Our eyes locked, and I hoped he went in for a kiss again. Instead, he said, "I was coming after you anyway, but if you're saying you want me too, I need you to know there's nothing I won't do to make sure you feel safe with me again."

I didn't realize how much I needed to hear him say that until he said it. That was much better than a kiss. Cupping his cheek, I gave him one on the side of his mouth. Because I wasn't ready to discuss how right he was about me not feeling safe with him after what happened with Sierra, I changed the subject.

"You still drink your coffee black with sugar?"

"Yeah. And you still take coffee with your cream?"

I couldn't help but laugh. Our tastes were the exact opposite when it came down to coffee. Mine was always light and sweet, and his was black with just a touch of sugar.

"That's the best way to have coffee and you can't tell me otherwise. Now... what happened with Sierra?"

"Aight, so you know I met her at a bar the night you broke up with me." I nodded my confirmation. "I was hurt and frustrated that you weren't willing to put in the work anymore, but I knew that was your choice, and I would never do anything to intentionally make you unhappy. If you felt like we were growing apart, I planned to honor that." He paused. "Sierra was supposed to be a one-night distraction. The first time we had sex, I strapped up. We drunk more at the hotel bar, and I got so full of it I used less discretion than I normally would. That night, she became the second woman I didn't use protection with along with you, and I've regretted that shit to this day."

"Why? Have you been unhappy in your marriage?"

"It started before the marriage. You know she was acting crazy while she was pregnant..."

"Yeah, that's why I called things off before the wedding. It was hard enough accepting that you had a baby with someone else, but Sierra's drama just made it unbearable."

"That was intentional. Sierra is actually cool as hell on a platonic level. Well, she was. We found out True wasn't mine, and I agreed to stay with her because the other nigga wasn't 'bout shit."

That didn't surprise me. With Asylum's background, I would have been more surprised if he walked away from a baby than if he stayed.

"My initial plan was to just be there for True, but like I

said, Sierra was cool. She cut back on the drama, and we started a genuine friendship."

"How did that lead to me seeing a wedding invitation for y'all on Facebook?"

He shrugged and briefly avoided my eyes. "I felt like being with her was my punishment for hurting you. Technically, I hadn't cheated, and I didn't sleep with her and get her pregnant on purpose, but still. I allowed my anger to guide me, and it fucked me up. So since I couldn't have you, I settled for her. The marriage was cool in the beginning. Even when I didn't want to be with Sierra, True made it worthwhile. Regardless of if she's mine or not, she's mine, you feel me?"

I nodded my understanding and he continued. "So, we ended up getting to a point in the marriage where I was unable to fake the funk anymore. The respect I had for her wasn't enough to keep me. I never loved her romantically. I only loved her because she was the mother of my child. When that stopped being enough, Sierra started going extra hard to spark some romance between us. It worked for a while, but there was always something between us that made me feel like I couldn't trust her fully and that I shouldn't devote myself to her altogether."

He paused again, taking a sip of his coffee. "To make a long story short, on our last anniversary, she said something to the effect of... it was crazy how much she did to have me, and I've never appreciated how much she loved me."

"What was that supposed to mean?"

"I asked her that, and she was tipsy and loose at the mouth. She admitted to lying about True possibly being mine. Sierra was pregnant when we had sex. That's why she asked me not to leave to get more condoms. When her nigga told her he didn't want a kid, she figured she'd pin the baby on me."

"Wow. Now that's some scandalous shit."

Asylum laughed, though there was nothing funny about his situation. "Right? I was pissed at her because I felt like her scheme was the reason I lost you. Not only did she lie about the paternity, but she was acting crazy as hell, making us have more issues. I told Sierra the baby was the reason you and I had called off the wedding, and she said she hoped it was mine so it wouldn't be in vain."

Asylum scoffed. "All this time I've been with a woman that I've never been in love with punishing myself for losing you, and her ass knew all along her baby wasn't mine. It hurt most because I probably would have still been in True's life if she would have been honest with me because I love kids and hate when a parent abandons them. But she cost me you, and I never let her forget that. I guess she got tired of me giving her the cold shoulder and telling her I was only staying with her until True turned eighteen, so she left."

"I can't see how any woman could leave her child, especially because a man doesn't want her. That's crazy. Do you think she's coming back?"

"Honestly, I don't know. I thought she would, which was why I hadn't signed the divorce papers. I felt bad about her going to such an extreme and figured maybe I could ease up. Then you came back into my life and... though I hate the reason behind it... I can't help but wonder if it's a God wink. If I'm finally going to have the chance to make things right with you."

That was a lot to take in, so I didn't respond right away. We both sipped our coffee in silence until several minutes had passed. As much as I loved the idea of being with Asylum again, I had to be honest with both of us.

"A lot of time has passed, Sy, and I'm sure we've both changed. Plus, with everything going on with Trey, I don't think I'd be able to focus on another relationship."

With a soft smile, he took my hand into his. "People change and grow. It's a part of life. I want to experience this version of you and grow through life together. As far as your ex is concerned, I'm going to handle that. If you would prefer to wait until I do to agree to allowing me to pursue you, I'll respect that. But like I said earlier, I was coming after you anyway, and I'm not going to let him ruin that."

All I could do was sit there with a goofy grin while he ate his cheese pastry. If he wanted to work to get me back, I wouldn't stand in his way. I hated hearing how Sierra had orchestrated things to work in her favor, and I hated hearing a young girl was now without her mother. As much as I loved the idea of her staying away, I prayed that she'd come back for True's sake. It was clear True meant a lot to Asylum, so I couldn't imagine how hard this was for him. If she did return, it would have to only be for True. This time around, I wouldn't give her my man so easily. Hell... she couldn't have my man at all.

Asylum

*S*weetheart: *I don't think I said it yesterday, but I'm sorry Sierra left you. With your history, I imagine that would be triggering. I also apologize for giving up on us so quickly. You asked me to wait until the DNA test was done and I didn't. I shudder thinking about how differently our lives would have been if I'd waited those last three months. On the bright side, True has you, and from what you've shared... she needed you more than me. I'm here if either of you need me for anything* ❤

I reread Dauterive's text. I hadn't been intentionally ignoring her. She sent it about two hours ago, and I wanted to respond to her in person. Doe shared that she was working from home until things cooled down with Trey. Unfortunately, I didn't see that happening. When a person started exhibiting this kind of behavior, they didn't just stop. They had to be stopped with jail or death.

Trey was MIA. I had someone sitting on his house 24/7 and he hadn't been there for the past three days. His neighbors saw him leave but not return. He hadn't been to his family's Fortune 500 Company, either. I had a plant at his office who agreed to let me know if he came to work for a fee. He also gave me access to Trey's email.

Before going to pick True up for our day together, I stopped to grab a few things for Dauterive. When we were together years ago, I never went to her empty handed unless the visit was impromptu. Even then, it was nothing for me to stop and get her a rose or an entire bouquet of them. Back then, she used to keep the dried petals in large vases all around her dorm and apartment. I wondered if she'd do that now?

After texting her to come to the door, I headed that way. When she opened it, a slow smile spread across her lips.

"Hi," she greeted me softly.

I took in the loose-fitting burgundy two piece set she had on for a brief moment before taking her by the waist and pulling her into me. She gasped, but it turned into a moan when I lowered myself and connected her lips with mine. Feeling her tongue swirl around mine after so many years felt like I was kissing a woman for the first time. Everything about her felt like the first time. Having her in my arms... on my lips.

It was supposed to be a quick peck, but with each quiet sigh and soft moan she released, it made it harder to release her. The kiss was slow and exploratory as we made up for lost time. My hands lowered to her round ass, squeezing it, and using it to pull her closer. My dick was getting harder by the second, and I had to force myself to pull away—otherwise, I'd have her palms pressed against the door while I reacquainted it with her pussy.

"Wow," she whispered, eyes still closed as she gripped the hem of my shirt.

"I know," I agreed, licking my lips to taste the remnants of her left behind.

Her eyes fluttered open as I pushed her hair out of her face. The golden blonde mane with black roots was styled in a crimped fashion that reached her armpits. I loved her hair, but I hated when anything obstructed me from seeing her beautiful face. My eyes shifted from her honey brown eyes to her plump pink lips. To avoid kissing her again, I put some space between us.

"Thank you for taking accountability for your part in our breakup. Thank you for forgiving me for mine."

Her head shook as she took my hand into hers and pulled me back into her space. "There was nothing to forgive you for, Sy. You didn't cheat on me. We were broken up. You tried to do right by me *and* Sierra while she was pregnant with who you thought might be your child. I'm the one who didn't have the will to stick around—"

"And that was your right," I interrupted to say. "It wasn't fair of me to ask you to wait for that. I know it was hurting you to watch me potentially have a baby with someone else. I should have let you go, but I loved you too much. That was selfish of me, and for that, I apologize."

Dauterive stood on the tips of her toes and wrapped her arms around me after kissing the tattoo of her face on my neck. Her petite, slim frame allowed her to be eye level with my chest without heels on. Holding her made me soften against her. I always felt whole when she was in my arms. Hell... when she was in my life.

I wished I had the emotional intelligence back then that I had now. If I did, I wouldn't have slept with Sierra. I would have understood where Doe was coming from and gave us both grace and space to process how we were feeling and move on from there. I kept telling myself it didn't matter because we had a chance now, but still. All the time wasted of us apart led to her being with an unstable man that she now needed to be protected from. What she said in her text message had been sticking with me though. True did need me, and if I was able to have a life that included them both, I'd be a very blessed man.

"Oh, I got you something."

Leaving her on the porch, I went to grab her gifts from the passenger seat which included her favorite chocolate and candy, a bouquet of red roses, and a Pandora timeless pavé cuban chain bracelet. It worked in my favor that Trey's family business was in Germantown by the Pandora store.

At the sight of everything in my hands, she gasped before giggling. Her hands went to her cheeks and eyes widened as she grinned.

"You didn't have to get me anything, babe."

"Making up for lost time."

"Thank you." After taking the items, she gave me another hug. "I missed you. I missed this—being with someone that makes me feel loved and wanted. You're amazing, Asylum, and I hope you haven't forgotten that."

"It seems like you didn't forget words of affirmation is my love language either."

Her head shook as she chuckled. "No, I didn't. I know physical touch was a close second for both of us, but no. It was words of affirmation for you and quality time for me."

"That's why I wanted to respond to your text in person so I could spend a brief moment with you, sweetheart. I'd already promised to spend the day with True but..."

"Go on, babe. I can imagine she needs even more attention and nurturing now. I appreciate the gifts and you stopping by."

"You sure?"

"I'm positive."

"Aight, well I'll call you tonight once I've gotten her settled in if that's cool."

"That sounds perfect to me."

Placing her hand on my chest, she lifted to the tips of her toes and gave me a quick, tender kiss. My eyes scanned the back of her frame as she turned to go back inside. Dauterive was slim, but she had a nice round ass that I couldn't wait to smack while I dug in her pussy from behind.

Running my fingers down the corners of my mouth, I pulled in a shaky breath to compose myself. I'd need more discipline than ever to keep from moving too fast. It was hard having boundaries with someone that I loved with no bounds. No conditions. I knew this woman better than I knew anyone else and vice versa. It felt foreign to take things slow with her. But she was worth it, and I had to keep telling myself that.

"I AM NOT this man's woman. I'm his daughter." The disgust on True's face made me laugh. It was clear she was way too young for me but asking if she was my girl was the waitress's way of getting my relationship status. She'd been flirting with me the entire time she served us. Since I wasn't sending much play her way, she became bolder to check my temperature.

As amusing as True's response was, it made me get a little emotional hearing her call herself my daughter. Up until now, she called me her stepdaddy and herself my stepdaughter. We'd gone from Mr. Sy to Daddy Sy. Sierra and I were cool with True calling me whatever she wanted;

it was her inconsistent ass daddy who made sure every time he had her that he reminded her he was her father... not me.

"Oh, I'm sorry." She looked between us. "She's a beautiful girl, but she must look like her mama."

True's head shook as she buried her head in her phone. She had been very possessive of me since she was a toddler and hated when we were out and women flirted with me.

"Yeah, she does."

"Are you... married?"

Technically, I was. The divorce had been filed and I was waiting for it to be finalized now that I'd signed and had my lawyer submit it on my behalf. Once the judge signed and processed it, I would be a single man again, though I was confident that wouldn't last long.

"Yeah, I am."

"Oh." Her voice lowered when she asked, "Happily?"

"Miss Lady, let me get that ticket up off ya so I can get my baby girl home."

She gave me a tight-lipped smile before nodding and walking away.

"Ew, she was so desperate and that was *not* cute."

"You remember that. Don't ever go harder for a man than he goes for you." After taking a sip of my water, I doubled down with, "Matter of fact, make sure the man you with likes you more than you like him."

"Why?" she asked, looking up from her phone.

"If he likes you more, he'll do whatever it takes to keep you because he won't want to lose you. If you like him more, he'll take advantage of it and get away with anything you let him."

"Did Mama like you more than you liked her?"

I didn't lie to True, but there were some things I withheld to protect her or her mother's image. At this point, I was done trying to spare Sierra.

"Yeah, she did."

"Hmm…" Her head nodded as she picked up one of her fries. "That makes sense."

"How so?"

"You never really seemed happy like my granddaddies or like my uncle is with his wife."

I laughed a soft laugh. "I wasn't. I never should have married your mother, just being honest."

"Then why did you?"

"Because of you." I pinched her cheek and she smiled. "I saw you and held you in my arms and loved you instantly, unconditionally. So… I tried to make a relationship work with your mom so I could be in your life, but I should have just been her friend."

Sadness covered her face, and her eyes watered when she asked, "Are you going to leave me like she did and make me go back to my daddy? I don't want to live with him, Daddy Sy. I want to stay with you."

"Baby girl," I almost hummed, pulling her into my side for a hug. "I'm never going to leave you. I promise."

Sierra left True with me for a reason. She may not have wanted to stay here and fight to keep me as her husband, but she knew I was a damn good father. No one was going to take True from me… especially her deadbeat ass sperm donor.

Dauterive

The incessant ringing of my phone woke me up after it took what felt like forever to get to sleep. My parents took a quick trip to Nashville, and having the house to myself allowed me to blast my music, drink a bottle of wine, and stuff myself with snacks until I passed out. With a groan, I felt around the bed for my phone. I wanted to let it ring, but on the off chance something was going on with them or my sister I needed to be aware. My eyes squinted at the brightness of the screen. My dad's contact photo was of him on the beach for their last anniversary.

"Hello?" I answered, sitting up in bed.

"Get out the house." My heart dropped instantly, and whatever sleepiness made it difficult to wake up was gone. "The camera alerted us that someone was at the door. He came inside. Your mom is on the phone with local police, but you need to get out—now."

"OK," I whispered, getting out of bed as quietly as I could.

Though I wanted to believe it was Trey and that he wouldn't hurt me, after the fire, I wasn't willing to take that chance. It could be a complete stranger trying to rob them and they didn't know I was here. Regardless of who it was, I didn't want them to find me in this house!

I didn't bother going to my closet for a full outfit. Instead, I grabbed the robe that hung on the back of the door. Not even bothering to put on any shoes, I slowly opened the door, cursing under my breath when it creaked. I made my way down the hall and looked down the stairs before tipping down them. The moment I rounded the corner of the stairs and reached for the front door, a pair of arms wrapped around me.

It truly startled me, forcing me to yelp as I tried to fight him off. After shoving me into the wall table, he slung me onto the floor and tried to straddle me.

"Help!" I yelled, trying to kick him wherever my feet would land.

His hands wrapped around my neck, making it impossible for me to breathe. Wiggling underneath him, I looked around for a weapon. My eyes landed on the broken vase that was originally on the wall table. To distract him, I flailed my legs, shifting his eyes there. Reaching to the right, I grabbed a piece of the vase and tried to stick it in his neck. He moved at the last minute, causing me to slice by his collarbone.

"Agh!" he yelled, scooting back and holding where I'd cut. It began to leak instantly.

Gaining my footing, I grabbed the gold statue from the floor and tried to hit him in the head with it, but he ran out of the house. I quickly locked the door behind him, though that didn't make me feel safe because he'd picked the lock to get inside.

I grabbed my phone with a shaking hand and rushed to the garage. Once inside my car, I locked the doors and cut the car on with the spare key I kept in the garage.

"Dauterive!"

At the sound of Daddy's voice, I looked down and saw that he was still holding on. "He's gone," I told him, winded.

"Where are you now?"

"In the garage. I nee—whew. Let me call you back. I need to call Sy."

"Alright, baby. We're on our way back now."

"Don't end your trip for me. He's gone and I'm sure Asylum will have somewhere else for me to go."

"Still, we're on the way back."

Nodding as if he could see me, I rested my head on the headrest. So much for my peaceful night of sleep.

I WAS grateful Daddy installed security cameras after the note. I was even more grateful I was able to cut whoever it was with the glass. It had his blood on it. The police had come and gone, taking it for evidence. If it was Trey as we suspected, a warrant would be issued for his arrest immediately. A part of me was praying it wouldn't be him, but if it was, at least this would get him out of my life temporarily.

After packing a few bags, I left with Asylum. He was pissed because he had no idea where Trey had come from. He hadn't been to his home or job. As he drove me to his home, he talked to someone named Merc. They were discussing a potential FBI associate that could track Trey's movements after hours better than they could. I appreciated the effort Asylum was putting into finding him, and I did feel safer being with him.

It took us about forty minutes to get to his home. It was gated and on several acres of land without a neighbor either way for half a mile. There was a guard at each corner of the gate plus two at the front of it, which I loved.

"Wow," I mumbled. "I take it providing protection makes you a target in some way?"

"It does. If a person is wanted bad enough some people will do anything to get to them, including coming after anyone helping them. Aside from that, I take pride in protecting anyone who comes to my home. And now... that includes you."

As Asylum nodded at the men in front of the gate, he told me, "I always have six guards here. My windows are bulletproof and they along with the door have iron that can be dropped with a remote or voice activation that are impenetrable. I have several cameras and motion sensors. I don't watch the cameras all day, so you'll still have privacy. I have them set up to scan any person who approaches the home that is not in my customized system. So I won't get any alerts about what you're doing, just if a stranger comes to the property. This is the safest place for you to be."

I already felt that but seeing all the extra precautions he'd taken made me feel even more safe and secure.

"Thank you, Sy. I feel better already."

"I would have offered my place to you after the fire, but I didn't want you to think I had ulterior motives in trying to get you here. Plus, there's True. I didn't know how comfortable you'd be with my daughter around."

His daughter.

I loved that.

I loved the devotion he had toward her.

Not only did it make him a better man in my book, but it was also sexy as hell.

It was crazy how time and maturity changed a person.

There was a time I hated the thought of dating a man who had kids. Now, it was a turn-on.

"As long as True is comfortable with me being here, I'm good. And I know we agreed to take things slow; I also know you're going to protect me. I trust you to do that here without it rushing what we have going on romantically."

"True's a good kid. She is a little possessive of me, but when she can trust that people have good intentions, she's very warm and kind. And as far as we're concerned, we always used to let things flow. I don't see why that has to change now."

I agreed and we got out of the car. He took my bags inside before giving me a tour. The six-bedroom, four-bathroom home was traditionally built, but he'd added some extra protective measures that were pretty cool, such as a bookshelf that led to a panic room and cabinets and fireplaces that held weapons.

When we were done with the tour, he showed me to the guest bedroom I'd be staying in. I appreciated him being a gentleman, but I wanted to sleep with him. I wouldn't say that, though. Not tonight at least.

"True!" he yelled, and not long after, the prettiest chocolate drop with long knotless braids hesitantly made her way inside. He wrapped his arm around her shoulders and pulled her into his side. "This is..." Sy paused, staring at me with a comfortable smile. "This is my sweetheart, Dauterive, but everyone calls her Doe. She's going to be staying with us while I find a bad man that's been trying to hurt her."

"If that's OK with you," I added quickly. I never wanted

a child to feel as if they had no say around me. Even if adults made decisions for them, I liked for them to know they had a voice to be heard.

"So she's in danger, Daddy Sy?" True asked.

"She is, and you know it's my job to help anyone in danger. She's a little special though because I like her a lot too."

With a wide smile, she looked up at him. "More than she likes you?"

I watched their exchange curiously. He nodded and chuckled. "Way more than she likes me."

Seemingly pleased with his answer, True walked over to me as I sat on the edge of the bed. She extended her hand for me to shake.

"Hi. I'm True."

"Hi, True. I'm Doe. It's nice to meet you."

"You too. How do you know my daddy?"

Her cute little voice and inquisitive smile made my heart skip a beat. "I almost married your daddy years ago. He was my favorite person in the entire world."

She looked back at Asylum. "Why didn't you marry her, Daddy Sy? Didn't you love her too?"

"I loved her more than any-fucking-thing," he admitted, eyes locked with mine. "That's why I had to let her go."

Swallowing hard, I gritted my teeth to keep my eyes dry. This night had been exhausting already, and this moment was adding on to my emotional jadedness. Asylum must have sensed that, because he told True to give me some privacy so I could unpack and get ready for bed. A quick tear slipped down my cheek as soon as I was alone. I had no idea how this had become my life, but I was grateful Asylum was back in it.

I<small>T WASN'T AS</small> easy as I thought it would be to go to sleep, so I decided to make myself a snack of apples and peanut butter. Even with me feeling as safe as I did, I still had flashbacks of what happened at my parents' home. It was almost five in the morning. They'd made their way back to Memphis, and after surrendering to my insistence, they agreed to stay with Dallas. I wanted them to get the locks changed and an alarm as well. Dallas suggested a guard dog too, but Daddy had a few guns and he felt they would be enough.

I hadn't even thought about them in the heat of the moment, which was why people said to try and stay calm during moments like that. I passed their bedroom where a gun was before going downstairs, and it completely slipped my mind. That was bothering me too.

The sound of slippers on tile alerted me to Asylum's presence before his voice did. As his arms wrapped around my waist, he said, "Couldn't sleep?"

"No. Did I wake you?"

"Nah. I couldn't sleep either."

After he placed a soft, wet kiss on my neck, I turned in his embrace. "Why not?"

"Having you so close yet so far away was driving me crazy."

I nodded my agreement with a smile. "Same."

"Why didn't you say anything?"

"I didn't want to impose. I'm already staying in your house. I didn't want to ask to sleep in your bed too."

"You don't have to ask. Whenever you want to sleep with me, just come."

"OK."

Asylum placed another kiss to my neck before leaving me alone in the kitchen. After finishing my snack, I headed back upstairs. He'd left his door open, but the lights were off. I went inside and closed the door behind me, then I made myself comfortable in his bed. Asylum wrapped his arm around me and pulled me onto his chest, and I couldn't stop the smile. He placed a kiss on the top of my head, tightening his grip around me as I tossed my leg around him.

"Damn." He chuckled. "I feel like I'm about to go to sleep already. You give me God's rest."

I wanted to ask him if he meant that, but there wasn't a need for me to.

Asylum never lied to me… even when it would have better benefited him to do so. He'd always been open and expressive, not subscribing to that toxic lie about men not being in tune with or not knowing how to express their emotions. Even if it wasn't natural, he'd learned how to do so, and I loved being with someone who communicated properly and didn't leave me confused.

Before I could respond, I heard the shift in his breathing.

"Sy?" I called softly, holding back my laugh when he didn't respond.

This man had fallen asleep already.

Asylum

T hree Days Later

I'D HAD the best sleep of my life for the last three nights. Well, two nights. When we finally went to sleep when she first got there it was well into the morning. I had a few people working to track Trey. Unfortunately, he only popped up when he popped up. I had a link in the FBI tracking his phone and credit cards, but they weren't coming up with anything.

I was hoping he could put an alert out for his face, so if he was spotted on any city cameras they would be notified. Because he was doing this after hours and off the record, he could only do the search for select timeframes. So far, nothing had come up. Wherever he was laying low, he had what he needed to survive while there... which made me believe he was possibly staying with a family member, but they all said they hadn't seen him.

I didn't have the manpower to put someone at the

house of everyone who knew him, so I was forced to wait for him to show his face. Even when he did that, we would have to act immediately. If he went to another hiding spot and we were unable to follow him, he would get away again.

Even without knowing where he was, I was confident that Doe would be safe because she was at my place. I could tell she was starting to get antsy, so I planned to take her out tonight. It was bad enough that she had to work from home, and I didn't want her to feel trapped.

While I waited for True to get out of school, I stopped to check in on Haley. I hadn't seen her since the party where she and Antonne announced their engagement. I was truly happy for my friend. She'd been in love with Antonne before her heart told her. It was clear for everyone around them to see. Their path to each other may not have been easy, but from the looks of it, it had been worth it.

"Sy," Haley called, lifting two more dresses for me to choose from.

I didn't mind when she asked for my opinion on her outfits. I had practice with her in preparation of what True would have me doing. Now that Sierra was gone, I questioned if I'd have to do it all myself. That was the thing about being a girl dad. True didn't give a damn about me being a man when she wanted me to take her to get her nails done and get mine done too. She didn't care about me looking out of place at her tiny table for a tea party. To her, I was simply Daddy Sy. Even without being her blood, True never made me feel like I was anything less than an extension of her.

"The red one," I told her. "What is this for anyway?"

"Me and Stink are going on a trip before Friendsgiving. You're coming, right?"

"Yeah, I'll be here. Or is it going to be at Kahlil and Honey's place?"

"I think it'll be here since they hosted last year. Or Supreme and Nicole might host it. I'm not sure yet."

"Did you know Nicole and Doe were best friends? All this time we've been running in the same circles but never catching each other."

"I didn't, but it appears it was finally time for you to catch your girl. How's she doing anyway? Is she getting along well with my girl?"

A smile spread my lips and I nodded as I thought about Doe and True. "She's good and they are getting along well. They've been doing dances from TikTok and they cooked together yesterday."

"What? I know True ate that up."

"You know it. Sierra hated when either of us were in the kitchen with her, so True was in heaven last night helping Doe fix dinner."

"Aww, I'm sure that was a cute moment."

"It was. I took pictures." I pulled my phone out while Haley walked over to me. The sight of several missed calls from Selena alarmed me. Had she heard from Sierra? After showing Haley the pictures I'd taken of Doe and True, I excused myself from her bedroom to return my ex-mother-in-law's calls. The divorce had officially been finalized, and Sierra and I were no longer married.

"Hello?" Selena answered.

"Hey. You good? Have you heard from your daughter?"

"I'm good, and I wish, but no. Bobby is here, and he said he wasn't leaving until he talked to you."

"Did he forget he has my number?"

She chuckled. "He said y'all need to talk face to face."

"Aight, let 'em know I'm about to be at 'em."

"OK, but please, Asylum... keep the peace."

I didn't agree. Peace would be determined by Bobby's actions. If he wanted to have a civil conversation about Sierra or True, we would do that. If he was going to be on some bullshit, I would handle that too. Since True was born Bobby hadn't liked me. For a while, he appreciated and respected the fact that I was taking care of his child. I think being looked at as a deadbeat was too much of a hit to his ego. He tried to step up and do more, but because it wasn't sincere, it was never consistent.

I wasn't a keep track kind of man, but out of True's twelve years of life, I was the one that was at every doctor's appointment and school event. I was the one that paid for every birthday party and Christmas gift. Whatever she needed financially I provided. When she had issues at school, I handled that.

Even when she went to his crib for the weekend or a holiday break, I made sure she was straight. His girlfriend had several kids that he was taking care of to appease her, and I knew their asses was getting damn near twelve hundred a month in food stamps... Yet I had to send True with money for them to feed her while she was there.

The nigga had never earned my respect, so how I handled him was up to him. I could be as good or as bad as a person's actions allowed me to be.

"I'm 'bout to head out, Ley. I'll talk to you later, aight?"

"Alright! Everything OK?" she checked, making her way down the hall.

"Yeah. Bobby wanna talk, so I'm about to go see what's up."

"Oh Lord. Please don't hit that man again."

I chuckled as I gave her a hug and told her goodbye. Things had only gotten physical between us once. He'd come to one of True's birthday parties with some liquor in his system, thinking he could show out. I laid his ass out with one punch, and we hadn't had any tumultuous issues since. Something was telling me he was about to be on one because Sierra was gone, so I mentally prepared for that as I drove. It took me about twenty minutes to get to Selena and Wayne's house. When I pulled up, he was leaning against his Infinity with a cigarette hanging from his mouth.

He favored Rickey Smiley. He was tall and lanky like him too. After tossing his cigarette, Bobby met me halfway in the driveway.

"Wassup?" I asked.

"Where in the hell is Sierra? Selena and Wayne won't tell me shit."

"They can't tell you something they don't know."

"Fuck is that supposed to mean?"

I pulled in a deep breath. "It means we don't know where Sierra is."

"How long has she been gone?"

"Just under two weeks."

"And y'all didn't think to tell me?"

I chuckled. "Tell you for what, Bobby?"

"I need to know what's going on with the person taking care of my damn child."

"I'm taking care of her, and she's just as good now as she was before her mama left."

"And you don't know where she is?"

"Nigga, did I fuckin' stutter?"

Bobby rolled his tongue over his teeth and took a step back. I was trying to be patient, but I hated when a person asked the same question expecting a different answer.

"You got until the end of the week. If SiSi ain't back, True is coming with me."

"OK. You can have her this weekend. I'm cool with that."

"Nah, I mean for good... or at least until her mama come back."

I stared at him for a few seconds before laughing. And I mean... it was a damn good laugh. The more I laughed, the more he frowned.

After I composed myself, I told him, "You can barely take care of True for a two-day weekend. How do you expect to keep her for longer?"

"That ain't got shit to do wit'chu. That's my child, and if her mama done disappeared, she belongs with me. How I'm 'posed to know you ain't did something to SiSi? How I'm 'posed to know she's safe wit'chu?"

Now that line of questioning made me get serious real quick. "I don't like what you're insinuating, so we're going to end this conversation now. But let me make this clear." I closed the space between us, and I saw the moment he inhaled and held a deep breath. Even though I knew legally I couldn't stop him from getting True, I told him, "She's not living with you. Now or ever."

"Contrary to what Sierra has let you believe, that's my child. If her mama ain't back by the end of the week, she's coming with me."

"You gon' come get 'er?" I asked, unable to keep the cocky grin from taking over my face.

"Nah, but the police will."

Chuckling, I headed to my car as I told him, "Let 'em come."

Dauterive

N icole and I decided to take it easy this afternoon. After brunch with unlimited mimosas, we crashed in her bed and were now watching a *Law and Order: SVU* marathon. I couldn't take another moment in the house. As nice as it was, and as good as it felt being with Sy and True, I was going stir-crazy. Being told I couldn't leave a place and having that control removed had been driving me crazy. I knew it was for my safety, but I just needed to breathe. Last night, Sy said they hadn't been able to get a hit on Trey, so he was hiding somewhere. He didn't know how to find me at this point, so I truly believed I was safe.

"How long before Supreme comes back home?" I asked her.

"I'm not sure, why?"

"I want to be out his bed before he gets here."

She chuckled. "Why? So he won't sit on you like last time?"

"That's exactly why!" I laughed myself.

I loved her husband and his brother like they were my brothers. Elite and Supreme were cool with Antonne, but because of my marriage, I kept my distance. Trey was insecure and didn't believe there was nothing sexual going on between me and my male friends. Whether they were married or dating, he refused to believe there was nothing or hadn't been anything between us. That should have been my first sign that he wouldn't be faithful.

I didn't take into consideration that his insecurity was him projecting because he could never be friends with a woman and not try to have sex with her. So for the bulk of our marriage, a lot of my friendships suffered. That was why three years had passed since I last saw Antonne. But now that we were back in each other's lives, we were cool like no amount of time had passed. Witnessing the changes in his life and heart was a beautiful sight to see, and I was so glad I no longer allowed my ex-husband to keep me from that.

"He said he was going to stop and see Baby Supreme, so he'll be gone for a while. He swears that's really his child."

"How's that going for you? I know you've always wanted kids and he didn't, which is weird because he's great with them."

She released a sad sigh as she nodded. "It's tough, I'm not gonna lie. That's also why he won't be in a rush to come home. We've been having some issues…"

At the sound of someone knocking on the door, we both sat up in bed.

"Are you expecting someone?" I asked as she reached to grab her phone from the nightstand.

"Nope. Let me check the camera to see who it is." When she chuckled and shook her head, I was even more curious.

"Who is it?"

"Go answer the door. It's for you."

"How is it for me? No one knows I'm here," I said as I climbed out of bed and stepped into my slides.

It didn't take me long to get to their front door, and when I opened it and saw Asylum standing behind it with a frown on his face, I shook my head.

"How the hell did you find me?"

Sucking his teeth, Asylum stepped inside the house and ignored me. "Supreme here?"

"Asylum." I tugged at his arm to get him to face me.

"I thought I told you to stay at the house? Do you know how dangerous it is for you to be out right now? We agreed until Trey was secured, you'd lay low."

"I *have* been laying low, and I was bored."

"I know, that's why I was going to take you out tonight."

"I couldn't wait that long," I whined, feeling my face form a pout. Usually I wasn't difficult, but between my racing thoughts, not going to my office, and being stuck in his beautiful home... I needed an escape.

"Dauterive..."

Uh oh. I knew he was upset or disappointed when he called me by my actual name.

"Sweetheart, why didn't you at least call me?"

"I didn't want to bother you. And how did you find me?"

"I tracked your location through your phone."

He said it so nonchalantly I couldn't help but laugh. "You put a tracker on me?"

"Nah."

"Then how did you track me?"

His expression finally relaxed as he smiled. "You don't

need to know all that. How much longer do you plan to be here?"

"I guess I can leave now since you've tracked me down."

After chuckling, Asylum placed a kiss to my forehead. "Aight, cool. Tell Nicole I said hello. I'll be waiting for you outside."

"Okay," I agreed before doing as he said. I trailed Asylum home, and I was unable to deny how cute it was that he pulled up on me. At least I knew if something ever happened to me, he'd be able to find me. That extra layer of security made me even happier to have him.

When we made it back to his place, I waited until we were parked in the garage and heading inside to tell him, "Sorry if I made you worry."

"It's cool. I really need you to not do that again. I don't have eyes on Trey yet, but he might have eyes on you and your people. If he comes after you again and you can't defend yourself…"

The fact that he couldn't even finish his statement had me stepping in front of him and taking his hands into mine.

"I'm OK. Right here, right now, I'm OK. There's no reason to even think about that."

His head shook as he cupped my cheeks. After pecking my lips a few times, Asylum rested his forehead on mine.

"I just had to face the reality that I'll be losing True soon. I can't lose you too."

"What happened, babe?"

We walked to his bedroom as he told me about his conversation with Bobby. I hated that this was happening. Even with us knowing he had no legal claim to True, he was more of her father than Bobby ever was. If Bobby *did* try to take her, there was no doubt in my mind that wouldn't have a pretty ending.

I suggested he take a shower to relax, and as much as I wanted to join him, I went into the guest room. He shared with me that his divorce had been finalized, which made it easier for me to open myself up to the possibility of us. And it wasn't a matter of thinking he'd treat me like Trey did. Sy was the safest man I'd ever been with.

I think what it boiled down to was a hesitance to allow my issues to become his. Asylum already had a lot on his plate with Sierra, True, and now Bobby. With everything going on with Trey, I didn't want my mood swings, fears, and toxic ex adding stress to his plate. Even though I was confident our time together would lead to us finally getting our forever, I was glad he agreed to continue to take things slow.

Asylum

When an ad on Facebook popped up letting me know the balloon festival was in town for the week, I decided that would be a good thing to do with True and Doe before it got crowded this weekend. I appreciated Dauterive wanting to include True in our plans for the evening, even though I told her I would make tonight all about her. After sharing with her what Bobby said, I was still committed to focusing on her tonight. But I couldn't lie and say I wasn't glad I didn't have to. The lingering possibility of True leaving me any time soon made me want to cherish my time with her.

I'd go to war with God behind True. I knew it would never come to that because He gave her to me. He was also aware of what I was capable of, so I could only pray He spared anyone who tried to come between us.

"Can I ride one more ride before we go?" True asked me.

"Yeah, but stay over here so I can see you."

"Yes, sir!" she agreed before racing toward a ride that

would spin her and lift her in the air before rapidly dropping down.

"Have you been enjoying yourself?" I asked Dauterive, taking her hand into mine. She seemed to be, but I wanted to ask anyway. Since she didn't have any kids, I wanted to make sure she was really OK with splitting her time with me. It wouldn't be like this always, but it was definitely an adjustment to get used to.

"I have. You were right, she's a really good kid. That's my lil friend forever now."

That made me happy. "She took to you very quickly, and that says a lot."

"I was really worried about how she would feel about me being there since I'm not her mom. She told me I made you happy and that because you liked me more than I liked you, she was OK with whatever this is we're doing."

"Yeah, we had a little relationship talk the day I came to see you at your parents' house. She knows that you make me happy and that's all she really cares about. Plus, the longer Sierra stays away, the angrier she gets. I keep tryna tell her I'll help her release it, but she's entitled to feel what she's feeling, you know?"

"She'll come to you in her own time, I'm sure. How are you doing with that, though? I was really worried about her being gone triggering you."

I didn't respond right away because she was right, Sierra leaving True *was* triggering. My father was never around, and my mother left when I was nine. She left me with my grandparents to raise me. *They* were my parents. Eventually, my mother started coming around more in my late twenties. The damage had been done by that point. I tolerated her for my grandparents, but I never acknowledged her as my mother.

For quite some time I struggled with insecurities and a sense of inferiority over her abandoning me. I felt like I wasn't good enough for love. It didn't matter what my grandparents said or did, it took years before their love started to heal me. By the time I met Doe I was in a better place, and being chosen and loved by her only healed me more. I think that was why I took her breaking up with me so hard. It took me back to that feeling of being abandoned and rejected. I wanted someone who wanted me... and that night... Sierra wanted me.

Hell, for years she has wanted me. But because I didn't feel the same about her it didn't soothe my soul the way I needed it to. I shared that with Sierra and that must have been the final straw for her. I guess she finally realized there was nothing she could do to make me love her the way I loved the woman whose face was tattooed on my neck.

"It was triggering. Having you with me during this time has grounded me. I'm able to detach and remind myself not to put my trauma onto her. All I can do is love her and make sure she never feels the rejection I felt. I want her to know I will always choose and want her, even if Bobby tries to make sure I can't have her. True will always be my baby girl, and she will always have a home with me."

Doe stepped in front of me and wrapped her arms around me. Resting her chin on my chest, she puckered her lips, and I wasted no time lowering myself to her for a kiss.

"I'm proud of you," she said before kissing my lips again. "And I want you." She gave me another kiss as I lowered my hands to her ass. "And I will never abandon you. I'll be here as long as you want me to be."

Moaning against her lips, I had to resist the urge to pick her up and wrap her legs around me. "You're making it harder and harder to not make love to you, sweetheart."

"The more I'm around you, the more I want you to."

"You want me to make that happen tonight?"

"When True isn't home. It's been a while and I don't want us to have to hold back."

"Mm…" Squeezing her ass, I lowered myself to her for another kiss. Her lips tasted sweet like the cotton candy she'd eaten earlier. Between rides and games, we'd pigged out.

I wasn't sure how long we stood there kissing and holding on to each other, but it was long enough for True to get off the ride and go on two more. When she made it back to us, the sound of her oohing and giggling was what caused us to pull away. She stood there with a wide smile that she tried to cover with her hand, looking from me to Dauterive. It was a way that I'd never seen her look at me and her mom before, and I wondered if us staying married knowing we didn't need to be together was doing True more harm than good.

We took care of her, but I questioned if we gave her a false perception of what love and marriage was supposed to be. The last thing I wanted was for her to be with a man who didn't really love her, barely liked her, or just tolerated her for whatever reason.

As we headed out, I considered if I wanted to tell True about her father's plans. I decided not to and to wait until the weekend to see what he would do. If he wanted to take her, I wasn't going to let her go without a fight, but I would make sure she was prepared.

～

HOURS Later

. . .

Up until tonight, Dauterive had been showering in the guest bathroom. I was cool with that, because I understood that even with us having a foundation that was already built, she still wanted us to take our time heading into this next phase. It seemed today changed things for us. Between me pulling up on her at Supreme and Nicole's home to the evening we spent with True and opening up about that, Doe was more affectionate than she had been since we first reconnected, and I loved that shit.

She'd left the bathroom door open while she showered, and as much as I wanted to join her, I showered in the guest bathroom that was in the hallway. All of the bedrooms were upstairs, so her guest bedroom was on one side of my room and True's room was on the other. That closeness had worked in my favor when it came down to making sure True wasn't watching things she shouldn't be or engaging in conversations on social media we didn't approve of. Tonight, that closeness would keep me from making love to the woman I loved most.

When Doe was done with her shower, she dried off and came to the door to ask me, "Will you come oil me down?"

Since I was seated on the bench in front of my bed, all I had to do was turn my head to look at her. She dropped her towel, exposing the caramel brown body that I'd made my playland years ago. The caramel brown body I'd reverenced years ago. I wasn't sure how long I stared, but it was long enough to make her giggle and put her hand on her waist.

"Are you going to stare at me all night, or are you going to come and do as I asked?"

Standing, I rubbed my palms together as I made my way over to her. Her perky breasts couldn't have been more than a B cup and they were calling my name. As much as I wanted to immediately palm them, I used my body to gently push her back into the bathroom then closed and locked the door behind us. Doe handed me the oil and stood in front of the mirror, watching me as I took my time oiling literally every inch of her body. I washed my hands after oiling her feet before directing my attention to her pussy.

"You're more beautiful than you ever were," I told her, gently strumming her clit. "You're perfect for me." Her eyes lowered, mouth parted, and breathing grew ragged. "I'm going to take full advantage of this second chance."

"Asylum," she moaned, clutching my shoulders.

Kneeling, I pushed her legs apart, then put the left one over my shoulder. Inhaling her scent, I bit down on my bottom lip as my eyes fluttered. Dauterive Jersey had *always* been an addiction for me. There was no doubt in my mind that if I indulged in her tonight, I wouldn't be able to let her go again. Not just because of the physical act of sex, but because of the oneness it would lead to. For the last thirteen years, it felt like I'd been walking around with half of my heart missing.

With her, it finally returned.

I kissed each thigh then cupped her ass and used it to tilt her hips. A low hum escaped me as I swiped my tongue over her opening. Her body locked the moment the warmth of my tongue connected with her slickness. I began my feast—licking and sucking and nibbling and blowing and breathing on the prettiest pussy I'd ever seen. Doe's grip on my head was tight as she released soft moans and curses. When she came, I lapped up every drop of her cum... determined to make sure no other man had the pleasure of drinking her essence after me.

Standing upright, I lifted Doe and set her on the edge of the sink. Our eyes locked as my middle and ring fingers made their way inside her pussy. The tight, hot, wet clutch of her walls against my fingers made my dick throb. A quiet whimper escaped her when I began to thumb her clit. I wrapped my hand around her neck and used it to press her back into the wall. The pressure I applied caused her to release a low, guttural moan that made cum ooze from my head.

"Be quiet," I commanded against her lips before kissing her deeply.

She returned the same fervent urgency of the kiss, holding my cheek and neck to keep my lips attached to hers. We kissed until she came against me, and each time she came, it was harder... and louder.

Doe unraveled the towel that was around my waist. Before I could question her, she requested, "Just the tip."

After releasing a hearty chuckle, I reminded her, "I'm supposed to be sayin' that shit."

"I don't need you to say it; I need you to do it."

"You know what you doing, right?"

Nodding, she stroked my curved length before putting it at her opening.

"Yes, babe. *Please*. Just the tip."

As I tapped her sensitive clit with my head, she jerked and squirmed. I could tell by the redness of her bottom lip that she was biting it hard to keep quiet. Before entering her, I slid my head up and down her opening, coating it with her nectar. Slowly, I pressed my way inside. She pushed at my stomach, keeping me from going all the way in.

Her low, lazy eyes were locked on mine as I stroked her with just the head. She was so wet, just that small amount of penetration had the sticky sound of her wetness slathering me filling the room. Labored breaths and hushed curses escaped us both as I kept a slow pace. Doe tweaked and pulled her nipples, keeping me in a trance. I put her ankles on my shoulders, tilting her and hitting her spot immediately.

The loud moan she released was my signal we wouldn't be able to do this long.

"Doe," I warned.

She nodded frantically, pulling in a shaky breath. The ridges of her g-spot swelled around me as her legs trembled.

"Asylum," she moaned, gripping my ass as she looked down at the connection of us.

I allowed my saliva to drop onto her clit before I covered it with my thumb. That was her undoing. I hadn't caressed her clit for five seconds before she was cumming against me. Losing all control, I pressed my way inside of her fully, covering her mouth with my palm when she cried out. The feeling of her walls pulsing against me as she came made me cum too. Her quiet whimpers behind my palm mixed with my low grunts. When I pulled out, our mixed cum seeped out too.

She pushed me back gently and got onto her knees, taking me into her mouth and sucking until I came again and had to push her away.

As she laughed, she stood on wobbly knees. I wrapped my arm around her waist to keep her steady.

"I said just the tip," she scolded softly with a pout.

"I did for as long as I could. You tested me worse than Satan tested Jesus in the wilderness."

That caused her to laugh harder as she wrapped her arms around my neck. "God, I love you."

Her widened eyes and opened mouth were proof that she hadn't meant to say that.

"Sorry," she mumbled, trying to quickly pull away from me.

I gripped her arm and pulled her back to keep her from running away.

"Hey," I called, tilting her head to look into her eyes. "Why you running?" I gave her a quick, tender kiss. "I've missed you every day that you've been out of my life. You never left my heart. I love you too, sweetheart."

Sniffling, she hugged me again, and I lifted her into the air to wrap her legs around me. For a while, I just held her... locking this moment in as a core memory. When I felt like we'd both come down from the emotional high, I carried her to the shower, and we washed each other before going to bed.

Dauterive

The Next Morning

CAN you bring me a Plan B pack?

🤖 ♣: *Yeah but don't take it yet. Let me get that pussy and fill you up for real before you do.*

I chuckled as I exited out of me and Asylum's text thread. While married to Trey, I took birth control because I didn't want to have a baby at that time. I'd realized getting on birth control was my intuition's way of telling me not to have a baby with that man. As soon as I left him, I got off, and I hadn't had sex with a man since—until last night with Sy.

The way he had me cumming with just his mouth, fingers, and tip was insane. We didn't even go all the way and I was sprung like I was years ago. Just one stroke had me wanting to take that man's last name.

It wasn't my plan to have any type of sex with him so soon, but I was tired of holding back. I knew Asylum more intimately than I knew any other man, and I gave that same privilege of knowing me to him. Regardless of the ways we'd changed over the years, our vibe and bond were still the same. I was excited to get to know this more mature and stable version of him, though, that I couldn't deny.

He'd left the house early this morning just after True went to school to run some errands. When he got back, he was going to get me out the house. I didn't know what he had planned, but just being in his presence was enough for me. I would be content riding around with him all day while he handled his business with my laptop while I handled mine. That was another thing I loved about being with Sy again. We were very intentional with loving each other in our love languages.

He was the only man I could spend hours with and never get bored or tired of being around. And now that we'd become more affectionate and physical, I was sure we'd be having sex more often. As much as I didn't want to get back on birth control I'd probably need to. Neither of us had stable enough lives to bring a baby into this world right now.

MY SHOULDERS HIKED and I cooed at the sight of what was waiting for me in the passenger seat. Asylum hadn't just picked up the Plan B pills... He also grabbed me a bouquet of flowers, a bear claw, and a chai tea latte from Panera Bread. I loved how he always thought of and considered me in small and big ways.

"Thank you, babe," I said, turning since he'd opened the door for me.

"You're more than welcome."

We shared a brief kiss before I moved the items and got into his Challenger. My eyes trailed him as he walked around the car. He was dressed pristinely in a navy-blue suit with a crisp white shirt underneath. I wasn't sure what he'd done this morning, but whatever it was, I was glad it granted me such a beautiful sight of him.

Asylum hadn't even pulled out of the garage before he was saying, "You don't wanna have my baby, Doe?"

His question made me choke on the sip of latte I'd taken. As he patted my back, he laughed. When he came inside and gave me the pills, he didn't mention anything about me taking them. It shouldn't have surprised me. He knew I'd try to avoid this conversation, so he waited until I was trapped in his damn car.

"Woah. You just dove right in there, huh?"

As I wiped my mouth, he chuckled. "You know I've always been direct and straightforward."

"Yeah, that's true."

He allowed the silence to linger for a while before saying, "Can I get an answer?"

"I didn't know we were there yet."

"There where? To talk about having a baby or actually having one?"

"Both." Chuckling nervously, I squeezed my thighs together and twiddled my thumbs as I stared out of the window.

"I know we're both fresh out of marriages we shouldn't have been in to begin with, so there's no rush. However..." Gently, Asylum turned my attention to him with his fingers under my chin. "We've lost thirteen years. I'm not going to intentionally try to get you pregnant any time soon, but I'm also going to cum in you every chance I get."

87

"You do realize that entire statement contradicts itself, right?"

"Not really." He massaged his chin and kept his gaze straight.

"How not, Sy?" I chuckled as I shifted slightly in my seat to face him. "You do understand if you cum in me every chance you get that I will get pregnant eventually, right?"

"If you don't take the necessary precautions to stop that from happening, I guess so." He shrugged, and I could barely take this conversation as seriously as I needed to because he was being so nonchalant. "You're the one that has a reservation about getting pregnant, so it'll be on you to get on birth control or get those Plan B pills in bulk. I'm cumming in that pussy, and if you get pregnant, I'm going to take care of you and our baby."

Rolling my tongue across my cheek, I chuckled with a shake of my head. "You're crazy."

"I'm quite sane actually." He took my hand into his and kissed it. "I'll buy you the world, but I ain't buying you that shit again. That's one thing you gon' have to always get yourself."

"Sy! We literally just reconnected. You don't think it's too soon for us to have a baby? I just got you back."

"Is that what this is about? You don't want to share me?"

Blinking back my tears, I shook my head. "No," I muttered. "I know we have lives and responsibilities outside of each other and we can't just lay up all day every day, but I'm really happy to have you back and I want to take full advantage of it. If I get pregnant..."

"That won't change anything," he interrupted me to say. "If you were to get pregnant, you'd be my wife before you became the mother of my child. I'd hire a full staff to make sure we had the help we needed to not lose ourselves in being parents. Our bond would still be my highest priority, and nothing or no one would come between that. You would be able to rest assured knowing there would always be times and days of the week that would be devoted exclusively to you. I will never put anything or anyone above you and make you feel like you can't have all of me that you want." He paused. "With me saying all of that, there's no rush for us to have a baby. What I guess I want you to understand is that this version of me goes with the flow and let's God decide. If we have a baby in nine months or nine years, I'm genuinely just as happy as you are to have you back in my life. Whatever comes with you, good or bad, I want it all."

For a while, I was speechless. Every worry and reservation I had, his words dissolved. Not just because I could trust his words, but because I knew I could trust his future actions. I released a shaky breath and dabbed the corners of my eyes.

"While I'm worried about us moving too fast, you don't even have us on a constraint of time."

His head shook as he chuckled. "Not at all, sweetheart. This is forever. We literally have all the time in the world. If you trust me and this flow... you'll enjoy where we take you. And to show you that I'm willing to compromise and accept how fast or slow you need this to go, I'll pull out... *sometimes.*"

That last part caused me to cackle. He smiled and licked his lips before shooting me a wink. God... I missed this man.

We ended up having a great day. He took me to check out his asylums and I was also able to go to my office. It was good to see Regina. I told her she could work from home like me, but she loved being in the office in case someone randomly stopped by. I'd been doing interviews virtually to bring in new clients and I was grateful my staffing agency allowed me to be so flexible. Still, I couldn't wait until this foolishness with Trey was over so I could return to a sense of normalcy that didn't require me to be home every day. Well, not home, but Sy's home.

When we left my office, Sy took me to go see his grandparents. Honestly, they were more like his parents, and he treated them as if they were. Yvonne allowed me to help her make bread, which she was known for. Every weekend people from their church and neighborhood stopped by for loaves of her fresh bread, but throughout the week, she reserved them just for her family. We ended up having lunch, and afterward, we watched a few old shows with Vernon. It felt like no time had passed, and I loved how warm and welcoming they were toward me.

By that point, it was time for us to head back home since True was about to get out of school. She was a fireball of energy and wanted to spend the night with one of her friends. Asylum confirmed that it was OK, then she packed a bag, and he took her a mile up the road so she could spend the night. I was very surprised when she gave me a hug and called me Ms. Doe before she left. Up until then, she'd been calling me Ms. Dauterive. It was something small, but it also made me feel like she was warming up to me even more.

We'd been spending a lot of time getting to know each other since I'd been here. We cooked and danced, and I even helped her with schoolwork. I loved the little family unit we had and how Sy incorporated God into their everyday lives. There were moments when thoughts of Sierra coming back would creep up, but since they were divorced, the most she could do was limit the time Asylum had with True. Though at this point, I honestly wasn't sure if the girl would ever come back. I still had no idea what her true reasoning was for leaving them behind, but I was happy to help, nurture, and give them love in any way I could.

"You almost ready, sweetheart?" Asylum called from the bedroom.

I was doing my makeup in the bathroom. We decided on a social club as our destination for the evening. It was fairly new, which I loved. They were known for small soul food bites, top shelf liquor, and a large dance space with a DJ, which a lot of lounges were lacking these days. At my age of thirty-six, I didn't care for clubs anymore, but I loved a good lounge and social club. Nothing was better than a night of drinks and dancing with friends to me. In tonight's case, dancing and drinks with my unofficial man. Though Asylum and I hadn't made things official yet, he was my safe space, and I was his sweetheart. For now, that was more than OK with me.

"HE'S PREDICTABLY IRRATIONAL," Asylum said to Daddy on the phone.

We'd had an amazing night at the new social club but when I got back in the car and noticed I had several missed calls and text messages from Trey I wondered what caused him to reach out to me. The last time I talked to him, it was the day he left the note at my parents' house and denied it. There had been a warrant issued for his arrest because it was his blood on the scene that night of the break in.

I realized he was probably calling because I'd posted pictures of myself before I left the house. Though I didn't post any of the ones I'd taken with Asylum, I did attach a cute caption that hinted at me spending the evening with a man. I couldn't wait to post the pictures of us that I'd taken at the social club, but now, I wasn't going to.

Daddy must have asked Asylum what he was going to do because he said, "I'm learning his ticks and patterns. He shows up when he's triggered by her actions of moving on. I had my connect tracking his location through his phone since he finally cut it on to call her. If I hear anything, I'll let you know."

After he disconnected the call, Asylum looked over at me and asked, "You good?"

I couldn't lie, I was a little shaken up by my conversation with Trey. Mostly because it showed how unstable he was becoming. He'd called again, and Sy told me to answer and put it on speakerphone so he could record the conversation on his phone.

"Hello?" I answered, heart beating wildly.

"You've moved on to someone else already?"

"Seeing as you cheated on me and got someone else pregnant, I really don't think that's something you have the right to ask me."

He breathed deeply into the phone. "You want me to cut her off? Because I will."

"I want you to turn yourself in to the police for breaking into my parents' home and trying to kill me."

Trey chuckled. "I have no idea what you're talking about, love."

"Yeah, you never seem to know what I'm talking about. Where are you, Trey?"

"Why? So you can send the police after me? You're even more disloyal than I thought you were."

"Are you dumb? You've set my house on fire, harassed me, broken into my parents' home and choked the shit out of me. If me wanting you arrested is disloyal, I'm about to be the most disloyal person you've ever met."

He was quiet for a while before saying, "I didn't do any of those things. If crazy things are happening now that you've divorced me, that's the universe's way of saying we belong together. Things will only get worse until you do right by me."

With a roll of my eyes, I taunted him with, "OK, Celie. Don't call me again. Leave me the fuck alone, Trey, before you get hurt."

"By who?" He laughed. "Your Daddy ain't the gangster he think he is. He won't shoot me."

"But I will," Sy replied.

"Who the hell is that?" Trey questioned through gritted teeth.

"Her man, and if you value your life, you'll stay away from Doe."

The line was silent for a while before he disconnected the call. For some reason, I didn't feel like that silence meant he was backing down. For some reason, I felt like that silence meant he was only getting started.

"Hey," Asylum called, brushing my cheek gently and pulling me out of my thoughts. "You know I'm not going to let that nigga hurt you, right?"

Clenching my jaw, I nodded before my head hung. "Yes. It's not that. I just... can't believe things have come to this. I don't see how I missed the signs."

"There probably were none, bae. He's clearly unstable,

and that kind of thing doesn't come out until you stop giving a narcissist what they want. There was nothing you did wrong or to deserve this, aight?"

Sniffling, I nodded, appreciating his assurance. I hated that I allowed his call to ruin my mood, but I couldn't get past it for the rest of the drive. Apparently, he had a fake page because I'd blocked him on my social media. After making all of my pages private, I blocked his number too. I knew there was a chance he could be tracked through his phone, but I didn't want to be triggered by hearing from him. He'd have to be found another way. I couldn't risk any more of my peace and sanity.

When we made it back home... to Sy's home... he told me to stay in the car for a while. I didn't know what he was up to, but I took that time to try and clear my mind. I prayed to God for peace and the strength to fight the battle I'd have with Trey and for the protection of me and other soldiers working on my behalf, with Asylum and my father being at the top of that list.

As Asylum opened the door, he said, "Aight, sweetheart, you can come in."

He led me inside by hand, and as soon as I saw the trail of tealight candles and rose petals, tears filled my eyes. They led to his room, where he had the most romantic setup I'd ever received. What I loved most was the picture of us from years ago that he'd had enlarged as a canvas print. It was hanging behind his bed as if it belonged there.

Rose petals were on the floor and bed, in the shape of a heart. The bench in front of his bed had chocolate covered fruit and champagne, along with several gift bags. Candles were on the nightstands and dresser, and balloons that spelled out *LOVE* were floating in front of the window.

"This is beautiful, babe. I love this."

His arms wrapped around me, and he placed a kiss on my neck. "I love you, Doe."

His declaration and the tender tone he used to give it had me turning in his arms to look into his eyes. "I love you." Sliding my hands down his chest, I told him, "Thank you for this. It's absolutely perfect."

"I don't usually do this kind of shit, but I'll let you soften me if it makes you happy."

With a giggle, I nodded and kissed him. "It makes me very, very happy." I looked back at the picture that had me in awe. "How did you even have time to have that done?"

"I've had that picture since we broke up. It was supposed to be a wedding gift I gave you. When we broke up, I decided to keep it. Something told me I'd need it one day."

"Asylum... Where have you had this? Not here, right?"

He chuckled. "Hell yeah. It's been in my man cave outside."

I chuckled and shook my head. He had enough land for him and Sierra to have smaller homes on the property that they used for their private space. I loved that for them. I'd keep Sierra's she-shed as she left it until the end of the year. If she didn't come home by then, I was tossing all her shit.

"I can't imagine how hard it was for her to see that... or even the tattoo of me on your neck. Did you get that back then too?"

"Yeah. I got it right after I found out True wasn't mine. It was my way of keeping you forever."

"You didn't plan to come after me?"

His head shook and expression saddened. "Nah. I felt like I didn't deserve you, though I'd always been good to you. I felt like your view of me may have been stained. I never wanted us to start treating each other differently, that's why I agreed to the breakup. With you, I had the healthiest relationship of my life, and I didn't want my fuck up with her to change that even more. So as hard as it was, I decided to let you go. I told God if He felt I deserved a second chance one day to bring you back to me."

"He did."

"Yeah... He did."

That made my tears rush back to the surface as I turned in his arms for another kiss. A kiss that led to him carrying me over to the bed. We undressed each other before tumbling into bed, where a long round of 69 led to my pussy wetting his face while I risked my life taking all of his dick down my throat.

On my knees, I braced for him as Asylum made his way behind me. He slowly stretched me, and the pleasurable relief of having him back inside had my back arching more and body relaxing against the bed. His strokes started out slow, giving me the time I needed to adjust to his length and girth. Sy was methodical with his strokes, creating a symphony of my cream against him that went from slow and steady to fast and upbeat. As his body slapped against mine, I begged him not to stop, though he seemingly had no intentions of doing so.

Ass slaps combined with back shots that had my body feeling paralyzed. He grabbed my hair and deepened my arch, unlocking me and commanding I take all of him. As I came against him, he hummed and gripped my waist, keeping me from falling into the bed.

As I lay on my back, Asylum made his way between my legs. He connected our lips as he slipped back inside me. Lifting himself, he wrapped my left leg around his waist and placed my right ankle on his shoulder. With slow, deep strokes, Sy kissed my calf with opened and closed mouth kisses that had my moans pouring as I leaked against him. He stayed in that position, holding my waist and keeping me open until I came again, then he lowered himself to me and kept both legs wrapped around him.

The deep tongue kiss we found ourselves tangled in increased my arousal. I held him close, never wanting to let him go.

"We don't need to be fucking like this," he panted against my ear, filling me with slow, deep strokes that tied his soul tighter around mine.

"You're right," I agreed breathlessly. "But please... don't stop."

And he didn't.

Each drugging, numbingly intense stroke made my pussy wetter and wetter. I released sizzling breaths as my toes curled. Clawing at his back, I returned his kiss with trembling lips. When I could no longer hold it back, I came. That time, he pulled out quickly and came too.

I loved his face as he came. The way his brows wrinkled and mouth hung open slightly before he tugged his bottom lip between his teeth... How he released a shaky breath and quiet hum. There wasn't anything I didn't love about this man... but witnessing him in such a euphoric state was one of my favorite things to love. To witness. To be a part of.

Asylum rolled over onto his side, causing me to do the same. He lifted my leg slightly and continued his strokes. If his stamina was how it used to be, he'd cum once more before he would be done. And as his medium paced sideways strokes filled me, I hoped it would be a while before that happened...

Asylum

Ten Days Later

IT WAS the weekend before Thanksgiving and I'd yet to hear from Bobby. I wasn't surprised because he was inconsistent as hell, but I didn't know if his threat of taking True could be forgotten about fully. Even with the unfortunate circumstances, I was enjoying having Doe here, and True was too. I told her that she could use the extra bedroom that had no furniture for a home office and Sierra's she-shed however she wanted to use it. I'd had both spaces cleared along with the closets of Sierra's belongings and I took them to her parents' home.

To my surprise, True had been going in both to feel closer to her mother. When she got home from school two days ago and saw them empty, she cried. I felt like shit, so I took her to her grandparents' house and let her pick out a few things to take with her. It sucked because she had to grieve a mother that was still living... and I knew that pain all too well. I suggested she start journaling about how she was feeling and that was helping. Lord knows I hated Sierra for putting us in this position, but we were dealing with it the best way we could.

Since True was with my grandparents for the weekend, I decided to devote my weekend to Dauterive. I planned to check in on my asylums every day before she got up to ensure I could keep my focus on her.

Today, I took her shopping before we came back home to cook and chill. I couldn't think of the last time I spent the weekend in the house chilling if True wasn't here. Even if I wasn't working, I'd be with family or friends to avoid Sierra. I loved being in Doe's presence and doing the simplest things with her, though.

The fireplace blazed as she cuddled against me on the reclining sofa. She had me watching some rom com on Hulu that I was sure she'd seen a million times. I didn't mind because she used to be a hopeless romantic. It seemed with time, or maybe the wrong partner, she got a little out of that... But I was trying to give her a space that was safe for her to return to her true self.

Wanting to get in her head about it, I asked, "How much do you think you've changed over the years?"

"In what ways?"

"All ways. With your priorities and morals, relationally, your goals for the future—everything."

"Hmm..." She shifted slightly but kept her head on my shoulder. As she played with my fingers, I kissed the top of her head. "My priorities are still the same. Family over everything. Then my career and friends. Now that you're back, you and True are up there with family. I still heavily prioritize having a good time and getting rest. If my mama didn't teach me anything, she taught me the best way to make the most of our short time on this earth. So I take great pride in my work-rest balance. My morals are still the same too."

She paused. "Relationally, I value friendships a hell of a lot more. I think that started because of my marriage. Things were best with us when I wasn't connected to my people, and I didn't like how that felt. At the end of the day, my friends were the ones that were there for me, and I appreciate them so much for that. Romantically, I still want the same things in a partner—loyalty, faithfulness, romance, fun, leadership, safety—but I think I might have changed a little. I'm a bit more guarded and less naïve. Well, maybe naïve isn't the right word. I used to be a hopeless romantic and believed love in all ways could heal and conquer all but that's changed now. Loving the wrong man made me value it a little less, but being with you is allowing me to return to my old beliefs."

I shared the same with her, and our conversation continued. We talked about our plans for the future. Professionally, she wanted to offer more headhunting like services for larger companies. With how she operated now, the bulk of the positions she staffed were temporary or short term, but she wanted to start having contracted agreements with companies for permanent positions.

Personally, she wanted to continue to get to know me and True and allow me to indulge in this new version of her. We talked about children again and agreed to have one or two. We wanted to travel more, experience more, and work less. My asylums were my pride and joy, and I took great honor in the service I provided, but I did want to trust my team more so I wouldn't have to pull up daily.

We ended up talking for hours like we used to do back in the day. By the time we climbed into bed, I felt even closer to her, which I didn't think was possible. What made my heart yield to her even more was her asking if she could buy some things for True before she got back home. True loved Hello Kitty but she didn't want her room decorated with it because some of her cousins teased her about it being for babies. Instead, SiSi and I designed her room in pink, red, and white.

During one of their conversations, True showed Doe a purple Hello Kitty sign that she liked but didn't want to get because it wouldn't match her room. I wasn't sure why she didn't tell me because she knew I would have gotten it for her without her even asking, but I appreciate the fact that that interaction invited Doe to offer and do something for her that she didn't have to.

Instead of turning the last spare room in the house into a space just for her, Dauterive decided to turn it into a spa-like escape for the both of them. It would be purple and cream, and she'd have Hello Kitty items incorporated, including the sign that would be in True's corner. She was so excited as she told me about the ideas she had, and that shit made me love her even more. Even though I chose to love a child that wasn't mine, I knew that wasn't something everyone did. The relationship they were building filled me with pride and further deepened my desire to never let Doe go.

THE NEXT NIGHT

DAUTERIVE and I met up with Haley and Antonne for a night of pool and drinks. About two hours in, the entire crew had pulled up to join us, and I loved every minute of it. We took over the pool hall. As blunts and bottles rotated, conversations flowed. We danced, sang, and rapped, and I took great pride in having Dauterive by my side. She wasn't just my lover; she was my friend. I forgot how fun a relationship could be. How fun love could be. But I was glad to have Doe for the reminder.

She was seated against the wall. Nicole's arm was wrapped around her shoulders as she whispered something in her ear. Dauterive wasn't a heavy drinker, so by now, she was sipping her shots instead of knocking them back with the rest of the women that were drinking. As if she felt my eyes on her, she searched the room for me.

As she smiled and grabbed her phone, I wasn't expecting her to text me until I felt my phone vibrate in my pocket.

Sweetheart: You look so sexy. I can't wait to get you home.

Home. I love the sound of that. We can leave now if you want to.

Her smile widened as she stood and began to give everyone a hug goodbye. I chuckled, but I couldn't deny how good it felt to want a woman just as much as she wanted me. I said my goodbyes as well before we headed out to my truck hand in hand. Once we were inside, she said, "That was so much fun, but I'm glad I get to finally have you to myself."

"Agreed. The guys are cool. I'll have to chill with more than just Antonne, Elite, and Supreme more often." As I headed out of the parking lot, I asked her, "Do you need anything before we get to the house?"

"Food. All we have is healthy stuff. I want something greasy and cheesy."

Now that made me laugh. The refrigerator *was* pretty

healthy. We'd started meal prepping breakfast and lunch to save on time. Even though Doe was at the house all day, I didn't want her to feel obligated to cook every meal and clean. She was still running her business just like I was running mine. I wanted to make her life as easy and soft as I could, because doing that for her made me feel more like a man.

I took her to this wing joint in the hood that stayed open until three in the morning. It was the only place that stayed open that late, so it was packed from wall to wall. Because I'd done a few favors for the owner over the years, as soon as he saw me, he directed us to the private room in the back. The space was usually reserved for card games, but they thankfully didn't have any scheduled that night.

By the time we were comfortably seated at the round, brown four-person table, a hippy waitress by the name of Debra was making her way over to us. She was around my mother's age but looked as young as thirty-five. Her long, wavy hair was pulled up into a high plait that swung as she walked. I could admit I considered sampling her pussy over the years, but even with things being off with Sierra and I, I never cheated.

"Wassup, Asylum?" she greeted, but her eyes were on Doe. "Who is this pretty little thing?"

"This is Dauterive, but everyone calls her Doe. Doe, this is Debra."

"Hi," Doe spoke sweetly, eyes resting low from the weed she'd ingested.

"Hey, pretty. What can I get you to drink?"

"Kool-Aid."

Debra smiled widely. "What color?"

"Red or pink."

"You want any liquor in it?"

"Hmm... What kind you got?"

"Any kind you want."

"Jack?"

"Several. You want it straight or flavored?"

"You can put a little honey or apple in it. Whichever you got."

"I got you. And for you?" Debra turned in my direction. "Your usual?"

"Nah, let me get a glass of Hen."

"Ooh, you're going to have some fun tonight," she said to Doe, swatting her shoulder softly and making her laugh before she walked away.

"She's cute," Doe said. "I take it you come here often?"

"Yeah. Any time work calls for late hours I end up here."

"I know I've said it before, but I really admire what you're doing with the asylums. This fits you. Maybe it's because you've been doing it for a while, but you look more solid and settled in this role than you did when you were an officer."

"Yeah, that was never really the job for me. I knew I wanted to make a change and help people and that seemed like the best way to do it. This is truly my passion and purpose though."

She gave me a syrupy smile. "Living in your purpose makes you sexier too. There's something about an established man that's top tier. And when he's emotionally available too? Whew."

I laughed at her silly ass as I sat further in my seat. "I missed you, man. I've been good without you, but the difference you make in my quality of life is unmatched."

"I feel the exact same way about you. I've never been the kind of woman to need a man, but I've enjoyed their companionship and love. With you..." Her head shook as she shrugged. "You've always been at the top of my want list."

Our eyes remained locked, unwavering until Debra set our drinks in front of us. I was even more anxious to get her home now. It took about fifteen minutes for our food to be delivered. She got a cheeseburger, and I got wings. We quickly made our way home to shower and show each other with our bodies the meaning behind our words.

"Are you sure this is necessary?" Mama asked. "I want her to be safe, but this seems a bit... extreme."

"Nothing is extreme when it comes to her safety," Daddy said.

Though Mama nodded her agreement, she still looked to Asylum for an answer. After church yesterday, I received a text from an unknown number. It was a faraway picture of me and Asylum entering the church. Attached was a text that said I wasn't as safe as I thought I was. It was clear it was from Trey. Apparently he'd been waiting at places I typically went to. It seemed like the only place I could truly get away from him was Asylum's home.

It was Asylum's decision to get me a bodyguard. Not only would that allow me to move around more freely, but it would allow me to go places without him. Though we loved the time we were spending together, he didn't want me to only be able to do things with him—which I appreciated.

"Yes, the bodyguard is necessary. It will allow Doe more freedom outside the house and protection when she's not with me."

"Any leads on where Trey has been staying?"

"We've been tracking his location through his phone and IP address, however, whatever software he's using is keeping my source with the FBI from finding him. And as it stands, he's watching the places he knows she will be to taunt her."

"So what's the plan?"

"Trey might be smart and have money to hide but he's not about that life. If he was, he would have approached us yesterday. At this point, I believe he won't try to harm her while she's with me or the bodyguard. He simply wants to scare her. I'll let a little time pass to see if he'll work up the nerve to approach her. She will go on with her life regularly with the guard. If he doesn't make a move within a month's time, I'm going to draw him out by using her as bait."

"Bait!" Mama yelled dramatically, and as serious as the situation was, we couldn't stop ourselves from laughing.

"Yes, Mama, bait," he answered, trying to reel in his laugh. "But she will be protected. He will just think she isn't. She'll show up, seemingly alone, but me and Merc will be there. I'll handle it."

"And when you say handle it..."

His head shook. "The less you know about that part the better."

Her head bobbed and she swallowed hard. "OK, son."

"We're trusting you with our precious gem," Daddy said. "Please don't let us down."

Asylum took my hand into his. "I give you my word, I will protect her with my life."

They seemed to be pleased with his answer, because

they returned to regular conversation over pastries and coffee. This was probably my favorite part of being my own boss—having the ability to set my own schedule. I loved the mornings I was able to spend with my parents and not have to rush in to work.

After breakfast, Asylum took me to one of the asylums, where I met Merc. He told me that Merc would be with me when I needed to go out in the mornings, and a second guy, Bully, would be there when I wanted to go out in the evenings. I knew from the tour he gave me of his asylums that Merc and Bully were the men he trusted most with his business and his life, so it meant a lot to me that they were who he was using for my guards.

We said our goodbyes, then I headed to the office. I was happy to feel like I was finally returning to a state of normalcy. Merc checked the office thoroughly before making himself comfortable outside of my conference room. He advised I worked there instead of in my personal office since it had so many windows. In the conference room, there was no chance of Trey sneaking in and I would still have privacy.

As I settled in, Regina brought my to-do list for the day. Before getting started, I FaceTimed Nicole to make sure she was OK. Both she and Supreme had come to the pool hall, but I didn't recall seeing them talk to each other which was weird.

"Hey, boo," she answered with a wide smile.

"Hey, baby. What you doing?"

"About to go to a few department stores and look around for inspiration. Are you at the office?"

"I am. I have a bodyguard now so I can move around more freely."

"That's great, Doe! I'm in desperate need of a girls' night."

"Of course! Just say when and we can make it happen."

We talked for a few seconds more before ending the call, and I immediately got to work.

Five hours flew by before I knew it. I had three more interviews with potential clients and had also set up a meeting with a potential Fortune 500 Company to start staffing. Trey's family business was the first one I'd staffed, and I learned a lot about headhunting for million and billion dollar companies. As toxic as things got between us, I did appreciate the professional connections I made because of him.

There was a soft knock on the door, and I told Regina she could come in. "You have a delivery, but Merc has to inspect it first."

"OK," I agreed, standing.

By the time I made it to the front, Merc had the box open. "I won't open anything from the list of family and friends Asylum gave me. This, however, had no card."

"What is it?" I asked as I made my way over to him.

"Flowers and a note."

Merc handed me the note. It was from Trey.

Love,

It's good to see you returning to normal. Did your master let you out, or are you done hiding? Either way, I'll be seeing you soon.

. . .

"GET RID OF IT. All of it." I handed him the note and headed back to the conference room.

Asylum was right. Trey was definitely watching my normal spots and using his knowledge of my routines to his advantage. That was fine. I didn't think he'd approach me while Sy or one of the guards were with me, so I felt like we'd be playing this game for a month before I became bait.

Asylum

B lack Friday

WITHOUT HER HAVING to say it, I could tell Dauterive was nervous. Everything that she ordered for the spa had been delivered over the past week, so she took the time to get the room setup for her and True. I offered to help but it was something she wanted to do for True on her own and I appreciated and respected that.

"Sweetheart," I called, taking her hand into mine.

She looked up at me, nibbling her bottom lip. "Hmm?"

"Why are you nervous?"

"It's that obvious?"

We shared a soft laugh. "Yeah, it is."

"I just hope she really likes it."

"She's going to love it."

With a nod, Dauterive released a shaky breath. True made her way upstairs. We'd told her to meet us up here after she was done with her dessert. She looked between us skeptically and I could barely contain my excitement behind my poker face. I knew my girl, and True was going to absolutely love what Doe had done.

"What's wrong?" she asked, wrapping her arms around Doe.

Dauterive had gotten her love of affection from her parents, and she was passing that on to True. Sierra and her family weren't affectionate at all. The only time she hugged True was if she was crying or if days had passed since she'd seen her. Sierra did show her love in other ways though, and they had a tight bond. But because of that lack of affection, True was always hesitant with being affectionate toward anyone but me and my grandparents. That barrier wasn't there with Doe, and that was yet another thing I loved.

Doe was a safe space for True, just like she was for me. In my entire life, Doe was the only woman outside of my grandmother that I felt like I could be my true self with. And there were things I was able to share with Doe that no one else experienced. She would always say I was her safe haven and the man whose love drove her crazy, but she had always been mine too.

"Nothing's wrong, baby girl," I answered since Dauterive was looking at me to speak. "Doe did something for you. The both of you. You wanna see?"

"Yes," she replied, doing a little dance.

This girl was going to be a dancer or track star I was convinced. As soon as she learned how to balance her studies and practice, I would let her try out for them again. We'd tried track last year, but it was a bit overwhelming.

"It's OK if you don't like it, but I hope you do," Doe said, opening the door.

True hesitantly peeked her head inside. Her eyes widened as she gasped. Hands flying over her mouth, she looked back at Doe.

"You did this? This is so cool! Is that... that's the Hello Kitty sign I wanted!"

True raced over to her corner of the room, where the neon purple Hello Kitty sign hovered over a table where she'd be able to read, draw, do crafts, or whatever else she wanted. Doe had her corner set up on the opposite side for her reading and lounging. In the middle of the room was their nails and spa stuff, and on the back wall in front of the window was a small daybed. A large TV was mounted across from that on the opposite wall, and underneath, there were crates of games for them to play.

"What do you think?" Doe asked, twiddling her thumbs.

True jogged over to Doe and almost knocked her over from hugging her so hard. "I love it! Thank you, Doe!"

"Of course! I'm glad you love it. I was so nervous."

They shared a laugh as True looked up at her, though Doe's five foot five frame wasn't that much taller than True who was five-two. I had a feeling she'd be taller like her mother, who was five foot nine.

"Why were you nervous?"

"I didn't want you to think I was trying to take your mom's place or win you with gifts. I genuinely just wanted us to have a space where we can hang out together without your daddy bothering us."

True laughed as she looked back at me while I rolled my eyes.

"I like hanging out with you, Doe. This is going to be perfect. We're going to have so much fun! I can't wait to get started! When can I do your nails?"

"You can do them now. I'm not doing anything."

"OK, perfect! Go pick your color."

Doe walked over to the tall rack full of nail polishes. As she scanned the selection, I decided to give them some space to do their thing. My phone vibrated in my pocket, and when I noticed it was one of the guards at the front gate, I headed toward the door.

"Yeah?"

"Uh, boss, there's a guy named Bobby here and two police cars. You want me to let them in?"

"He ain't got no choice," Bobby said in the background, clearly not knowing who the fuck I was. If I said they couldn't get through, they wouldn't get through.

"Yeah, you can let 'em in."

I tried to remain calm, but my anger was brewing on the inside. "Doe!" I roared, needing her with me. She was probably the only thing that would keep me half calm.

She made her way down the stairs with concern covering her face. "Is everything OK?"

"That nigga came to my fuckin' house," I whispered, though True wouldn't be able to hear me.

"Who, Trey?"

"Bobby."

"How did he get your address? I thought y'all did drop-offs at Sierra's parents' house?"

"We do. So either she gave him my address or her parents did."

I didn't care about him having it because it was always guarded, but it was the principle of the situation. He hadn't earned the right to know where True was being raised because of how inactive he was in her life. I didn't want him thinking he could pop up at any point and mess with her emotions. She needed structure to limit her disappointment that came with being his child.

"Shit. Well... what are you going to do?"

"I wanna beat his ass. He brought the law to my shit, and I know he's coming to get my girl."

"Oh no. Sy..."

There was a knock on the door, and I didn't know what to do. The audacity this nigga had was blowing me. He could barely handle True for a weekend and now he wanted to be a full-time daddy. Their bond was shaky at best. I'd worry myself sick thinking about what she was exposed to while she was with him. He didn't even take care of his own child, but he took care of his girlfriend's bad ass kids. And if any of them put a hand on my baby I was going to jail for beating up a little kid.

Opening the door, I looked from one officer to another. Bobby was standing behind them with a wide smile.

"What?" I asked, not bothering to open the door enough for them to come in.

"I'm here for my daughter," Bobby said.

"Is True Biggims here?" one of the officers asked.

"Yeah, but she ain't goin' with y'all."

"You can't keep her here," Bobby said. "She ain't your daughter; she's mine. My name is on her birth certificate."

"You think I give a fuck about that shit?" I tried to get at him, but the officer that spoke stepped in front of me and put his hand on my chest. That immediately set me off. Pushing his hand away, I told him, "Don't put your fucking hands on me."

"Asylum, please," Dauterive said behind me.

"How are you going to get her to school?" I asked. "You're going to completely disrupt her normal routine because you a hatin' ass nigga. She don't know your woman or them kids because you don't get her enough, and now you expect her to be comfortable living there?"

"Mr. Matthews," the other officer said. "By law, we have to take the child. If anything happens while she's in Mr. Biggims care, you can open a case and file a petition for full custody."

"Y'all not taking her anywhere," I made clear.

"Then arrest him for kidnapping," Bobbi said.

"Mr. Matthews, please," the second officer said. "There's a right way to handle this but going against us isn't it."

"Here's right, babe," Doe said, stepping between us. When I didn't look down at her, she tilted my head by my neck and forced me to look into her eyes. "If you want full custody, you need to make sure a judge understands you're a better option than him. I know you don't want to let her go with him right now, but you have to."

Every inch of my heart wanted to go against them, but she was right. As much as I didn't want to, I called for True to come down. Just like she did upstairs, she went to Doe and wrapped her arm around her waist. Lowering myself to one knee, I gently gripped her arms and swallowed hard.

"Because your mom is gone, your dad wants you to stay with him."

She looked from me to Bobby. "You're my dad." My eyes squeezed shut as they watered. "Both of you. B-but I like living with you."

"I know, baby girl," I almost whispered, swallowing hard. Regardless of how hard this was for me, I had to be strong for her.

"It's time to go with Daddy," Bobby said. "Yo' *real* daddy."

"I don't want to." She was standing firm, and as happy as that made me, I knew it would also make this worse.

"You ain't got no choice," Bobby replied.

"Will you shut the fuck up and let me handle this?" I said through gritted teeth as I stood.

"I don't have time for this. Go get her shit for school so we can go. She got clothes at my house."

"I don't want to go, Daddy Sy!"

Bobby stepped between the officers and reached for her, and it took every ounce of self-discipline I had not to swing on him.

"I'm going to get you back, baby girl. I promise."

"I'll go get her things," Doe offered.

As she cried and reached for me, that shit broke me even more. By the time Doe returned with her bag, Bobby had picked her up and she was fighting in his arms. I couldn't stop myself from telling her, "Give 'em hell, True. You'll be back home soon."

My words sent her into a frenzy, and it made me proud to see her fighting to stay with me. I repeatedly told her I loved her and that I would have her back soon as her father carried her away—kicking and screaming. Once they all had swerved onto the main street, I headed to the fireplace in the living room. I entered the password for it to lift and retrieved my Glock and suppressor.

"Asylum..." Doe called hesitantly. "What are you doing?"

"I'm going to kill him and take her back." Her hand wrapped around my wrist as she stepped in front of me. I didn't want to take my frustration out on her, so I pulled in a deep breath before telling her, "Move."

"No. I'm not going to let you permanently ruin your chance to get her back."

"Dauterive..."

"Baby, I know this is hard for you, but I can't let you do this." I tried to walk around her, but she stepped in front of me again. "We have to do this the right way," she stressed. "You know this won't last long. He's going to bring her back in a matter of days. And if he doesn't, you'll take him to court. Let him show himself as unfit. If you kill him the day he got her, you're going to be the first fucking suspect." Her hand lowered from my wrist to the gun. "Please have a little control and let fate handle this like everything else. Please, babe."

Gritting my teeth, I shook my head as my nostrils flared.

Doe's grip around the gun tightened, and I allowed her to take it. She put it back in its place and closed the fireplace before leading me upstairs to my bedroom. I hadn't realized my tears were falling until she wiped my face before stripping me of my clothes. She held me and prayed for me as I warred with my emotions. It felt like it took an eternity, but eventually, the urge to end Bobby's life left me.

As she rubbed my head and hummed a familiar tune, she placed a kiss on my temple.

"You're my stabilizer," I told her.

"Hmm? What did you say, babe?"

Sitting up, I repeated myself. "You're my stabilizer. You keep me steady. If you weren't here, ain't no doubt about it... I would've went after that mane tonight."

"Well, I'm glad I was here. True needs you, and I need you too." Her lips connected with mine before she rested her forehead on mine. "We're gonna get her back, Asylum. OK?"

"I don't like this, Doe. I feel so exposed and vulnerable and not in a good way."

"What can I do to make it better? What can I do to make you feel as protected right now as you make everyone else feel?"

"You're doing enough," I admitted. "Just being here, keeping me sane, that's enough."

I pulled her into my chest, placing her head under my chin. This was going to be a long ass night.

Dauterive

E arly December

TRUE HAD BEEN GONE for a week, and Asylum had slipped into a state of depression. He was barely eating and sleeping, and I was really concerned about his mental wellbeing. Selena suggested he try and see True, but Bobby wasn't answering his calls. Asylum decided to pay them a visit, and I was worried about how it would end.

Selena had been recording her calls with True. Apparently, True wasn't being fed properly—none of the kids were unless they went to school that day. They didn't have full, balanced meals. All Bobby did was buy them fast food when he got off from work at night. His girlfriend didn't fix them breakfast or lunch, and he wasn't taking True to school. She said she'd been eating Pop-Tarts and chips throughout the day until he came home with fast food. On top of him working, he didn't really spend any time with her or try to talk to her while he was home. I couldn't

120

understand for the life of me why he'd even gone through all of this to get her.

I was scared of what Asylum would do to Bobby as soon as we pulled into the driveway of his home. It was small and looked like it wasn't big enough to fit five kids let alone two adults. I hated that True was dealing with this on top of the situation with her mother. The structure and love Asylum provided was what allowed True to handle not having her mother around. And now, she didn't have him either.

"Those phone calls are proof that they are unfit to keep her," I reminded Asylum. "They are enough to go downtown and open a case. Please don't let your anger make this situation worse."

"Aight," he agreed with a nod. "Stay in here."

I wanted to be close in case I needed to hold him back, but I didn't want him worried about me, so I stayed in the car. There was an Infinity in the driveway that I was sure belonged to Bobby. Selena told us he was off today, so there was no reason for him to not answer the door for Sy. I could tell he was losing his patience when he laughed. Next thing I know, this crazy ass man was kicking down the door.

I hopped out of the car and ran into the house behind him.

"Where the *fuck* is my girl?" Asylum asked, looking around the tiny living room space.

I assumed the woman braiding hair on the couch was Bobby's girlfriend. She looked like she'd seen a ghost at the sight of Asylum, and after what he'd just done, I didn't blame her.

"I-I don't know who you're talki—"

"True!" Asylum roared, heading down the hall. "Where she at?"

"Are you crazy?" I seethed quietly, almost having to jog to keep up behind him. "These people can say you're trespassing. You need to get out of this house!"

Opening doors one by one, Asylum didn't stop until he found Bobby in a room smoking. I knew he heard what was going on outside, so the fact that he was sitting there calmly irritated my soul.

"Where my daughter at, mane?" Asylum questioned, hovering over Bobby.

"I didn't know you had kids."

Bobby set his blunt down and stood.

"You think this shit is a game? What's this I'm hearing about you not feeding her or taking her to school?"

"Nigga, that ain't got shi—"

Before he could finish his words, Asylum's fist was connecting with his eye and mouth. The impact of the hits had him flying into the wall. By the time he landed on the thinly carpeted floor, he was knocked out.

"Getcho ass out this house *now*!" I roared, shoving Asylum toward the door.

"Somebody need to tell me where the hell True at. I'm not leaving until they do."

"I just called the police!" the woman in the living room yelled as we entered.

"I don't give a fuck about that. Where is True?"

"She's at Chuck E. Cheese with my kids and their grandma for my youngest baby's birthday. They'll be back tomorrow afternoon."

Not waiting to hear another word, Asylum stormed out of the house.

∼

Seven minutes later, we were in the parking lot of the closest Chuck E. Cheese. It was an assumption that they were at this one, and after we walked around for a while and saw her, it was proven to be true.

"True!" he called, gaining her attention.

At the sight of us, she immediately broke into tears. True ran toward us, jumping into Asylum's arms. Tears came to my eyes at the sight of their embrace. I could tell they both needed this.

"Daddy!" she sobbed, and that made his tears fall. Since I'd been around, this was the first time she left Sy off. "You came!"

"I'ma always come for you. I can't take you home today, but Daddy is working on it, okay? I promise this will be over soon."

"Yes, sir," she said through her cries.

I rubbed both their backs and wiped my eyes. When he put her down, she gave me a warm hug as well. We took in her appearance. She didn't look that much smaller, but I could tell she wasn't eating as much as she used to. The clothes she had on looked like they were way too small. Like they'd been left at his house over the years. Her hair wasn't neatly done like it was when she was with us... and the woman clearly knew how to do hair because she was braiding someone else's when we got there.

Asylum took a few pictures of her before they embraced again, then we left. I'd never felt so helpless before. Not even when I was going through my own shit. At least then I could fight my way out. With this, it felt like there was literally nothing I could do.

Asylum

One Week Later

EVEN THOUGH DOE said I didn't have to, I still wanted to take her out tonight. Not just because she deserved to still be a priority to me, but because spending time with her would give me a little relief. I'd been working like crazy to distract myself from the fact that True wasn't home and she'd been out the house a lot to avoid my absence.

I also wanted to thank her for holding things down for the past two weeks. I could admit that I hadn't been myself and I wasn't taking care of my responsibilities either. She made sure the house was clean and she cooked and forced me to eat even when I didn't have an appetite. This moment showed me that at my worst, I could count on her, and it made me want to make her my life partner and wife.

It felt like so many things were out of my control, but her love was keeping me steady... stable. Every day that passed without True increased my hatred of Sierra. I had no idea where she was or what she was up to, but she was the reason True was in an unstable environment, and I'd never forgive her for that. There was nothing she could say to justify why she left.

"How should I dress for tonight, even though we really don't have to go out?" Dauterive asked.

"Dress comfortably and pack a bag."

"Where are we going?"

"To the airport. We're going to pick a destination and fly there tonight."

"Ooh, this is going to be fun!" Her smile made me smile for what felt like the first time in forever as she clapped her hands and shifted her weight from one foot to the other. "How long are we going to stay?"

"As long as you want us to. It's not like we have anyone to rush home to."

I hadn't meant for my comment to ruin her mood, but it was the truth. She made her way over to me and cupped my cheeks. Doe pecked my lips until I softened against her smile. Squeezing her ass, I held her close.

"There's that beautiful smile again. I miss this version of you."

"I do too. And I'm sorry about this. I know you have your own shit going on. You don't need to be worried about all this."

"That's nonsense. I care about True, and I want her right back here with you. I'm glad I'm able to be here with you, and I'm here for whatever you need."

After another quick kiss, I released her so she could pack an overnight bag. Forty-five minutes later, we were heading out the door to the airport. While sitting in the parking lot, we decided on a flight to Houston, which was cool. At least we'd be able to drink enough for me to force myself to have a good time.

Because the truth of the matter was, I'd learned there were different types of love and joy, and one couldn't replace the other. Regardless of how great of a time I knew we'd have, thoughts of True would still be in the back of my mind. It was the same way when True was born and I couldn't stop thinking about Doe. As happy as I was to have True, I missed my Doe. Nothing could take her place in my life then, and nothing would take True's place in my life now.

THAT FOLLOWING Wednesday

"I CAN'T BELIEVE I let you talk me into this," I grumbled through my smile.

"You're going to love it when you see the pictures. I'm sure they came out great."

I'd let her talk me into going to JC Penny to take a random ass photoshoot. The poses we did were hilarious, and I was sure this was some shit I'd want to take to my grave. I couldn't lie, though, it was fun, and it made her laugh, and that was all I needed.

We ended up staying in Houston all weekend and we took a day trip to Dallas Monday before our nine a.m. flight the next morning. All in all, the trip gave me more relief than I thought it would, and I definitely needed it.

I appreciated the effort Doe was making to try to keep me in good spirits. It had a positive effect on me. The more she took care of me and made sure I didn't stay in my head, the more clarity I had, and the easier it was for me to think of ways to expedite the process of getting True back. Apparently, there was an iPhone that had no service but had Wi-Fi and all the kids used it for social media. She'd been messaging me on Facebook sporadically, and that helped too.

My only hope was that True would be back by Christmas and we could take pictures as a family. A half an hour later, the pictures were ready, and they were just as crazy looking as I thought they would be. We died of laughter as we looked at them. I had to admit, this would be a core memory for me. I'd cherish the photos forever.

"I can't wait to show everyone these," Doe said as we headed to the car.

"Don't show *nobody* that shit."

"Asylum! I'm showing *everybody*. We look *good*."

She pointed at the picture of her on my back with her arms spread wide as we laughed, and the image made me laugh all over again.

"You are so beautiful. I can't wait to have a little girl that looks like you."

"After you give me a little boy that looks like you."

I wrapped my arm around her and gave her a kiss before opening the passenger door for her. Once we were inside, I checked my phone notifications since I left it in the car during the photo shoot. I saw that I had missed calls from my grandma, so I decided to call her before we left out.

"Hello?" she answered, clearing her throat in the process.

"Wassup, Ma? You called?"

"Can you stop by?"

"Is everything OK?"

"Yeah. Ya mama is here."

"And?"

"She wants to see you."

Chuckling, I shook my head. "I'm good on that, Ma."

"Do it for me, baby. Please?"

Releasing a long sigh, I hesitated to agree. I hadn't seen my mother in about four months, and I wanted to keep it that way. Every time we saw each other, it was the same thing. She'd try to make small talk and I wouldn't want to listen to a word she had to say. Then she'd get upset and try to make me feel bad for not allowing her to have more access in my life. To me, she gave up her access to me when she abandoned me. I didn't care if she'd come to her senses and realized leaving me with my grandparents to raise was foul. I'd forgiven her for it for my own sake, but I would never forget it or treat her as if it hadn't happened. I'd learned to live without her, and I hated when these visits came up and I had to deal with her trying to insert herself into a position she gave away.

"With everything that's going on with True, I'm really not trying to deal with that lady right now, Ma."

"You don't have to stay long. I made you a sweet potato pie. Just come over and get it, say hi, then you can leave."

"Aight," I agreed before disconnecting the call.

"Are you OK?" Doe asked, squeezing my thigh.

"Yeah. She wants me to come see her daughter and get a sweet potato pie."

She chuckled. "As good as Grandma Yvonne's pies are, I think that's a fair trade."

I didn't want to smile but I did because she was right. Grandma only made the pies for holidays, so the fact that she made it today meant she really wanted me to stop by. I offered to take Dauterive home before I did, but she said she was cool with riding with me. I genuinely didn't plan on being there long, so that was cool. Once I had my pie we could head home and call it a night.

When we made it to my grandparents' home, I wanted to keep the truck running to ensure I made a quick exit. Instead, I cut it off and decided nothing would keep me from making the woman that raised me happy, even if that meant playing nice with her daughter.

"You got this, babe," Doe said. "We can leave as soon as you want to. And if she gets out of line, I got you."

I'd told Dauterive about how toxic our conversations could get. Amber's selfishness and entitlement had a lot to do with why she thought it was OK to just drop me off with her parents and not return for years. In a lot of ways, Sierra reminded me of her. I hadn't realized I was looking for bits of my mother that I found in Sierra until she left True. The similarities might not have been what led to our first night together, but they were what made me feel attached to her during her pregnancy and after I found out the baby wasn't mine.

I used my key to let us inside. Immediately, jook joint music blasted from a YouTube playlist on the TV and the smell of soul food hit my nostrils. If Amber wasn't here, I'd stay to eat. Since she was, I would more than likely take a plate to go.

"There's my boy," GrandPops said as he stood.

"Wassup, Pops?" I greeted him as we hugged.

"Can't call it. Still tryna figure out how yo' funny lookin' ass got a woman as pretty as this."

"I guess the same way you got my grandma, huh?" I replied as he hugged Dauterive, causing them both to laugh.

After another minute or two of small talk, Grandma made her way into the living room. A young seventy-five years old, she came through strutting and dancing to the song that was playing, snapping her fingers. GrandPops did a quick two step with her and smacked her ass, causing her to blush like we hadn't seen him be affectionate toward her since the beginning of time. I laughed as I pulled her in for a hug.

"Thank you for coming, baby."

"Anything for you."

"Hey, Grandma Yvonne."

"Hey, my baby. Y'all look so... colorful!"

That got a hearty laugh out of us. We'd dressed in overalls with red and green sweaters underneath and orange Nikes. The beanies on our heads were blue and yellow. I was convinced Dauterive wanted to embarrass us for years to come with the pictures we'd taken earlier.

"Oh! Let me go get our pictures out the car so you can see."

"Y'all took pictures like this?" Grandma asked.

"It's a trend right now for some reason, Ma," I explained. "People get dressed crazy and take pictures in even crazier poses..."

My thoughts trailed off at the sight of my mother when she entered the room.

"Hey, Asylum," she greeted with a wave.

"Wassup, Sis?"

Grandma swatted my chest, but I didn't give a damn about that shit.

"What did I tell you about calling your mama that?"

"That ain't my mama; that's my sister. She let y'all raise me, so you my mama."

Throwing her hands up in a dismissive gesture, Grandma headed toward the kitchen. "Come on in here and get you some' to eat."

"Yes, ma'am," I agreed, prepared to walk past my mother as if she wasn't there.

She grabbed my arm. "Can we talk, son?"

"Na—"

"Sy," GrandPops called.

With a huff, I nodded my agreement. "Fix us some plates to go, Ma," I requested as I followed my mother out to the back porch.

We sat on opposite sides of the red velvet couch that was in front of the TV. Since I didn't have anything to say to her, I waited for her to talk. I couldn't look at her. She looked too much like me... Which was why I could never understand how she gave up a part of herself.

"Mama told me you're having some issues with your stepdaughter."

I didn't bother correcting her. There was no point in telling her True was my child even though she technically wasn't. She didn't even value her own blood enough to keep me, so how could she possibly understand me stepping up to raise another man's child?

"Yeah," was all I said.

"I'm sorry to hear that."

I nodded. I wanted to ask her why she left me. Maybe that would give me insight on what to say to True. That was one question she'd constantly asked that I didn't have a better reasoning for beyond she needed a break from life. Her response to that had been, "She ain't tired of resting *yet*?" It was never funny, but the innocence and feistiness of her question would always make me laugh.

"Hopefully she'll be home soon."

"I'll be praying for you." Chuckling, I shook my head. She smacked her lips. "You don't think God hears my prayers?"

"I don't know, man," I said, more amused than I probably should have been. "Is this what you wanted to talk to me about?"

"I just wanted you to know if you needed to talk about what was going on with True… I'm here for you."

"Yeah, because if anyone knows about abandoning their child, it's you."

"Come on, Sy. That was low."

"Not lower than what you did to me."

"Are you ever going to forgive me?"

"I already have. But just because I've forgiven you, that doesn't mean I have to deal with you. You brought me into this world and left mine for almost twenty years. You were gone longer than you've been back. That's a lot to deal with."

She sighed and looked at her palms as they rested in her lap. "Leaving you here was a mistake. No… It was a choice. The wrong choice. I know that might never matter to you, but I know that now."

"Why did you do it?"

She shrugged. "I was selfish. I felt like I wouldn't be any good for you at that point. I felt like I was failing as a mother because I was struggling so much. You would have had more security here, so I left. It wasn't because I didn't love you or didn't want to be your mother; I couldn't be anyone's mother at that time. I was barely able to take care of myself."

"Why couldn't you just get your shit together or say that? You didn't even warn me or say goodbye. You literally dropped me off over here like it was a regular visit and didn't come back for years!"

Amber took her time. She was careful with her words.

"I had been struggling for a while, Asylum. I'd tried to

get it together, but it just wasn't working. And I couldn't warn you or say goodbye because it was too hard. Had I done that, it would have been even harder to walk away from you."

I thought hearing her reasoning would make things make sense, but they only filled me with more questions that I was already too drained to ask.

Standing, I told her, "I got traumas because of you that I'm still working through to this day. You said you made a wrong choice, and I can respect that, but you gon' have to deal with the consequences of your actions, and that's not having a relationship with me."

Her head hung, and I wasn't sure if it was sadness or guilt. I didn't care either way. God Himself would have to soften my heart toward her. When I went into the kitchen, Doe and Grandma were making plans to have an afternoon of tea over the weekend. After grabbing my pie and our to-go plates, I gave Grandma a kiss on the cheek, and we said our goodbyes.

Dauterive

"You're getting lighter on your feet," Asylum said with his back still turned to me.

I could only chuckle as I continued toward where he stood at the island in the kitchen. It didn't matter how quiet I was, he seemed to always know I was around. I wrapped my arms around his waist and placed a kiss on his naked back.

"How'd you know I was coming?"

"I felt you. I smelled you. And I heard your toe pop."

That last part made me laugh as I stood next to him. When I saw what he was working on, my heart turned to mush. It was a pink and red gift box with all of my favorite snacks sticking out along with a bear, balloon, duo set of my favorite strawberry pound cake scented candles, and a card.

"Babe…"

I kissed his arm and rested my head on it as he put a bottle of wine inside.

"This is for the spa room. You haven't gone in there

since True left." Asylum tilted my head and looked into my eyes. "I want you to use it, sweetheart."

My head shook as I toyed with the tissue paper that hung out of the box. "I don't want to be in there without her."

"I understand that, but we don't know when she's coming back. You put a lot of thought and effort into that space. She would want you to use it." He slid the box in my direction and kissed the top of my head. "What are you still doing up?"

"Thank you for this. And I miss sleeping with you. I was coming to see if you'd be coming to bed any time soon."

It was a cheesy attempt at trying to get him back on a regular sleep schedule, but I hoped it worked. He still wasn't sleeping regularly since True left, even though he'd started to eat more.

"I can come hold you until you fall asleep, but if I can't sleep, I'm going to leave."

That was a start. I had a few tricks up my sleeve to make him not want to leave the bed.

"is there a particular reason you don't think you'll be able to go to sleep tonight?" I asked, pulling the card out of the gift box.

"Yes, and don't read that until after you've spent time in that room."

With a roll of my eyes, I nodded and set the card back in the box. "How about if I agree to utilize the room, you agree to stay in bed at least two hours before getting out if you don't immediately go to sleep?"

"This starts tonight?"

"Yeah." I paused, thinking maybe seeing his mother had something to do with his deepened state of insomnia. "Is this about Amber?"

When he nodded, I pulled out the chairs behind the island for us to have a seat.

"I thought things had gone OK when you didn't look angry as we left."

"I wasn't mad; I was..." He shrugged and twisted his mouth to the side as he processed his feelings. "Disappointed."

"In her?"

"In myself."

"Why?"

"I'm tired of going back and forth with her. Tired of rehashing the most traumatizing experience of my life. Tired of having questions and getting answers that only leave me frustrated with more questions. It's clear I'm going to have to tolerate her for a while, at least while my grandparents are still living. I guess I'm just drained from how much our interactions take out of me."

I didn't respond right away, giving myself time to fully process what he was struggling with.

"First, no one can make you deal with her. I don't care who it is. If dealing with her makes you this upset, it's OK to have that boundary of no contact to maintain your peace. Is it engaging with her in general that's the problem, or how you've been engaging with her?"

"It's how I've been engaging with her. I don't think I'd care about being in her space if we didn't have to talk about her abandoning me every time I was. I guess I'm just tired of reminding her of what she did and what it did to me."

"She doesn't need that reminder, babe," I told him with a soft chuckle. "Your presence is the kind that, without it, causes lack. I'm sure she regrets that decision more than you will ever know."

"That's what she's been saying. Tonight she finally told

me her reasoning behind it, and in that moment it wasn't a good enough reason to me. Hell, it's still not a good enough reason for me. But now that I've had time to think it over, I understand where she was coming from." He paused and released a slow breath. "Don't get me wrong, there's nothing in this world that would make me give my child to someone else to raise. I don't care how much I'm struggling, I'll figure things out and get help if I need it. But... I guess in her own way, that was her way of showing me love and making sure I was straight. She gave me to her parents because she knew they would be able to give me a better life. While I wish she would have stayed in mine, I can't fault her for keeping her distance if that's what she needed to do for herself in that moment."

"And look at it from this perspective: if she wouldn't have sent you there, you wouldn't have changed schools, gotten that scholarship, and met me. Then, we wouldn't have broken up and set the tone for your night with Sierra. Without that, there would be no you and True. And I honestly don't know how her life would have been with just her parents in it. I can't speak to Sierra's mothering while she was here, but if Bobby was the only father figure she had in her life, True would definitely be at a disadvantage."

"You're right," he agreed, taking my hand into his. "I heavily believe in fate aligning us for the paths God wants us to walk. Without that moment, we wouldn't be who and where we are today. As much as I hate the time we spent apart, I think it was necessary for us to become these versions of ourselves. So even though I hate what she did, it led to all the good that we have now."

"Which means..." I urged, leaning forward slightly and making him laugh.

"Which means I won't be so hard on her, but I still don't see us having a relationship."

"And you're gonna stop calling her your sister?"

He laughed, and the sound was like music to my ears. I loved the crinkles on the sides of his eyes and those straight, white teeth. Every version of Asylum was beautiful, but him happy was definitely my favorite.

"Bae!"

"Nah, you wrong for that, Asylum." I didn't want to, but I laughed. "Stop calling that lady Sis. Call her Amber if you don't want to call her Mama."

With a huff, he nodded his agreement as his laughter died down. Sucking his teeth, he grumbled, "Aight, aight. I'll ease up."

"Thank you." I pecked his lips. "I'm very proud of you."

His eyes scanned my frame. "How proud?"

"Proud enough to put you to bed."

As quickly as he hopped off the chair and picked me up bridal style filled me with laughter. He may not have been able to get to sleep on his own, but after I catered to his body and let him into mine, Asylum would be sleeping like a baby in no time.

THAT WEEKEND

I WAS TOO TICKLED over a drunk Haley. This was the first time I'd ever seen her drunk because she knew her limits. Instead of getting regular mimosas for brunch, we got what the restaurant called Macmosas which was champagne, orange juice, and vodka. She'd called Antonne telling him that she accidently got drunk, and he came to get her expeditiously. Nicole, Denali, and I had offered to get her home safely, but I think my friend just wanted to see Haley in this element.

As we all walked to our cars, we laughed as Haley waved and told us she loved us. Even with Antonne holding her up, she still managed to trip over her own feet and almost fell into a bush. He scooped her up and carried her to the car, laughing just as hard as we were.

"That girl is never going to drink anything other than wine and tequila again," I said, wiping the tears from my eyes.

"I know, right?" Denali agreed. I was glad she was able to get out. With her new baby, Elite and their kids were her top priority. I felt like I could only see my girl if I went to her house, which was understandable. If I had a new baby with the love of my life that had taken my two other children on as his own, I wouldn't want to leave home either.

"What y'all about to get into?" Nicole asked.

"You know I'm about to go back home to my baby," Denali said.

"I might go see my parents," I replied, looking back at Merc. He was alert and close but far enough away for me to feel like I was alone. "Sy is handling business with his asylums and looking into some old apartment buildings. He'll probably be gone all day."

"Apartment buildings?" Nicole repeated.

"Yeah. He's been talking about opening a couple of shelters in the city to go along with the asylums. Apparently, his intake research is showing him the bulk of the women that come to him are leaving abusive relationships or toxic families. He's thinking about separating the men and women and using the shelters for women and families."

"That's amazing!" Denali said.

"Absolutely," Nicole agreed. "Tell Bro if he needs help with anything to let me know."

"Will do." We all hugged and said our goodbyes before I told Merc about my next location. He jumped into his car, and I got into mine. Merc must have told Asylum we were leaving because about a minute into my drive he was sending me a FaceTime request.

I answered, and the sight of him with True almost made me run into the car in front of me.

"Oh my God!" I squealed. "Truuue!"

She giggled as she waved. "Heeey, Ms. Doe! I miss you!"

Tears were already threatening to fall as I alternated between looking at her and the road. I put my hazard lights on and pulled over into the right lane.

"I miss you too, baby love! It's so, so good to see you!"

"Come see me!"

"Where y'all at?"

"Her grandparents' house," Asylum said. "Merc has the address. Follow him."

"OK. I'm on my way."

Once I got back into traffic, Merc got in front of me and led the way. About fifteen minutes passed before we were pulling up, and Asylum was already outside. He must have been done with work for the day because he relieved Merc. Before I went inside, Asylum asked to speak with me and that was cause for concern.

"What's going on?" I asked, leaning against my car.

"Bobby dropped her off here indefinitely," he shared. I thought that would have made him happy, but his expression showed a different emotion. "Apparently his girl said she needs to be going to school because she can't take care of her and feed her all day and do hair." Asylum chuckled and squeezed the back of his neck. "Their water was shut off, so True was unable to bathe all last fuckin' week, Doe. And that ain't the worst of it." Sy paused and took in a deep breath. "She got welts on her back from a whupping he gave her because she was so upset over the living conditions that she cried and told him she wanted to go back home to her real daddy. Instead of him soothing her and defusing the situation like an adult, he argued with a child and got so upset he gave my girl a whupping for speaking the truth."

He released a bitter chuckle and ran his fingers down the corners of his mouth. "So she's staying here for a while, and he claims he's going to be randomly stopping by to make sure she's not with me. Selena is supposed to take her to school and make sure she's straight while Bobby gets some things in order."

"Wait, so he still plans to get her back?"

"Yeah. He wants her to stay here until the start of the new year. By then, he wants to have her transferred to a school out that way."

"And what about their living situation? I'm not judging anyone going through hard times but if she's not being fed properly and they have no water, she doesn't need to be there."

"I'm on the same fuckin' wave. They got roaches and shit too. And I'm not talking about just one. They have an infestation. She ain't even been able to rest because they be crawling on her and shit." His eyes watered as he looked away. "My girl has really been going through it over there." He wiped a quickly fallen tear. "My first mind told me to call CPS. All them kids'll get taken out that house but I didn't want to put them in that situation. Instead, I'm going to open the case first thing Monday morning. They will have a caseworker go check the living conditions and she will be removed from the home indefinitely. They may give them a certain amount of time to get it taken care of, but I have to get custody of her before they do."

"And what about the other kids?"

"By Monday, Selena said they will be staying with his girl's sister, so they'll be out the house. They won't be removed and placed in a foster home temporarily."

"Good." I clutched my chest as relief filled me. Though we wanted better for them, I knew he had a thing about kids being separated from their parents.

"Only thing is, I can't guarantee she'll be placed with me while the case is open and that she won't be returned to him. I'm cool with her staying here; I just don't want her going back there."

Silence found us for a while as I thought over any possible solutions.

"If I'm not mistaken, I staffed a woman in the juvenile clerk's office. If I did, maybe she can help." I pulled my phone out of my purse. "Let me get Regina to go through our files and see."

Lord knows I needed to have a connection in there that could do us this solid. True needed to be returned home ASAP, and if there was anything I could do to help make that happen, I was going to do it.

Asylum

M onday

THE SHOCK of my visit was written all over my mother's face. She blinked rapidly as she stared at me with her mouth hung open. It was the first time since she came back into our lives that I put forth the effort to see or talk to her. Chuckling, I lifted her chin to close her mouth.

"A-Asylum... come in," she offered, but I shook my head.

"I can't stay. I just... I wanted to say thank you."

Her head tilted and brows wrinkled as she clutched the door. "For what?"

"Giving me up."

Amber's body swayed as if my words knocked the breath out of her. I never thought I'd come to this moment, this perspective. After watching Bobby struggle to take care of his daughter and another woman's kids, I finally understood why my mother left me. His pride positioned him to do two things: not change for the better and keep a child he knew he couldn't take care of. That wasn't being a good parent; that was being selfish and not putting what was best for them ahead of his pride.

I thought back over my childhood with my mother and I could see her struggle. As a kid, it didn't faze me because that was my normal. For True, she hadn't had those struggles for the first twelve years of her life, so leaving me and going to Bobby was a complete shock for her. If I had to choose between the childhood I had with my mother and the childhood I had with my grandparents, my grandparents would win every time.

"I don't agree with how you did it," I continued, "But I'm glad you did it."

"Where is this coming from?"

I gave her a brief rundown of what transpired over the weekend before I ended with, "That's why I can't stay. I have to be at the courthouse at ten."

"I pray it works out in True's favor. And..." She paused and took in a shaky breath. "I'm truly sorry for how I left you, Sy. I could have put my ego aside and moved in with my parents to raise you and receive their help, but I was tired... and proud. I didn't want the responsibility anymore. I gave up because I felt like a failure." Amber took my hand into hers, and for the first time, I didn't immediately pull it away. "I'm proud of the man you've become, and I'm glad you're fighting for True the way I didn't have the sense to fight for you. Please let me know how everything turns out, OK?"

Before I could agree, she was pulling me into her arms for an embrace. For the first time since I was nine years old, I hugged my mother. I didn't expect it to affect me, but it did. The longer she held me, the weaker I felt. And before I

144

knew it, I was that nine-year-old boy crying and yearning for his mother all over again...

"YOU OK, DADDY?"

I looked over at True and smiled. I was a few minutes late for the hearing, but it didn't matter. Thanks to Doe's connections, we were able to get on Judge Wilson's docket as soon as the caseworker left Bobby's house. After hearing about the living conditions they were currently dealing with, he ordered the immediate removal of the children from the home. Bobby's girlfriend, Tamara, was allowed to keep her children at her sister's house... and True was able to come home with me.

There was no doubt in my mind that Doe was responsible for that. Usually, the kids would have had to be taken in by the state and a relative would have to be approved before the kids could go with them. I wasn't sure how she got one of her old hires to talk to Wilson on our behalf, but I would be eternally grateful for it.

It was temporary, but it was a start, and I was grateful to God for that.

Wilson gave Bobby and Tamara sixty days to improve their living conditions, otherwise, the children would be permanently removed from the home. He didn't even bother to show up for the hearing, so I wasn't sure how dedicated he would be to this process. Either way, I had to ensure that regardless of what he did over the next sixty days that True would be able to remain with me... at least throughout the week.

If he wanted her on the weekends like before, I was OK with that, but there was no way in hell I'd let him have her full-time. She had just started going back to school last week, and now, they were out for Christmas break. She'd missed several weeks of school and would be behind. I planned to go and talk to her teachers after the break to see what all we had to do to get her caught up. Between him not prioritizing her schooling and them not feeding the kids properly, the water being cut back on and roach infestation being taken care of would still make the place unlivable for True in my opinion.

"I'm good, just in thought. I'm happy you're home."

"Me too! I knew you would get me back no matter how long it took."

Her faith and trust in me made my soul smile. "Now this isn't permanent. For right now, it's just for the next sixty days, but I'm gonna do everything I can to keep you here. Even if I have to work something out with your father that includes him having you on the weekends. How would you feel about that?"

Shrugging, she looked out of the window and huffed. "I don't see what's the point of me going over there. We don't really spend any time together. It be so many kids over there he never focuses on me. And he always gets mad when I talk about you and Ms. Doe. I love him because he's my daddy, but I don't like being with him. I just want to stay here."

The judge had made it clear True's desires would be taken into consideration, but the final decision would be made based on what he thought was best.

"Well, I'll make sure I let the judge know how you feel, and you'll have the chance to as well."

She nodded and finally returned her eyes to mine. "Yes, sir."

We got out of the car and headed to the house. I didn't

tell Doe the good news because I wanted her to be surprised. As soon as we made it inside, True began her search for Doe. She found her in their spa room reading a book.

"Ah!" Doe squealed and stood, pulling True in for a bear hug. "Welcome home, baby love!"

"Thank you!" True laughed as Doe rocked her from side to side.

With both of my girls home, it felt like a nigga could breathe and rest easy after a very, very long time.

EARLY THE NEXT Morning

GROGGILY, I checked the time on my phone. I was so at peace now that True was home that I went to sleep early as hell. After dinner, I crashed. What was supposed to be me sitting on the bed for a minute turned into me sleeping until four in the morning. Doe stirred against me. I laid back down, not wanting to wake her up, but she was such a light sleeper that she woke up anyway.

"Hey, sleepy head," she said with sleep thick in her voice.

"Sorry for waking you up."

"It's OK. I'm just glad you finally got some sleep. What time is it?"

"A little after four. Try and go back to sleep."

"I'll probably go ahead and get up now. The sooner I get started with pairing clients with jobs, the sooner I'll be done with work."

"I was thinking we could go out of town for a little

while."

"You know I'm always down for a trip." She chuckled softly, and I found myself in awe of how I loved everything about this woman—even the way she sounded when she first woke up. "Where did you have in mind?"

"Somewhere kid friendly with stuff we will enjoy as well."

"I agree. After everything she's dealt with, True needs a good vacation."

"I know I said it earlier but thank you again for your help. If you hadn't stepped in, she'd be in state custody right now."

Her hand caressed my cheek. "I'm just glad I was able to help. I love you both, and I'm happy you got your girl back."

Though I couldn't see her smile, I heard it in her voice.

"I'm happy I got *you* back. Even with the craziness going on with Bobby and Trey, having you back has increased my happiness and peace tenfold." I kissed her neck and cheek as my hand lowered to her ass. "I hope you know I'm not letting you go this time."

"I don't want you to let me go ever, babe."

"I'm glad we're on the same page," I told her before connecting her lips with mine.

Our kisses led to me removing my clothes and pulling her onto my lap. As she lifted my shirt off her body, I lifted her frame and slid her down on my dick. The quiet moan she released at our connection was always the start to my favorite song.

Sitting up, I caressed every inch of her body I could touch as she rode me slowly. Licking and kissing her nipples, I made my way up her chest and neck to her lips. As our kiss deepened, her pussy grew wetter and wetter. There was something about becoming one with Doe that felt so intimate it was spiritual. I would never get tired of experiencing her in this way.

Low hums escaped me as she came. Feeling her walls leak and throb became too much to bear. I hadn't cum inside of her since the first time we reconnected, but that was about to change if she didn't get up. My toes curled and stomach clenched as my dick throbbed inside of her.

"You need to move, sweetheart." I moaned as I gripped her waist. "I'm about to cum."

Her right arm was wrapped around my head as she bounced against me. "I don't wanna stop."

"You know what that means, right?" I confirmed, sticking my fingers in her mouth.

Once she wet them, I wrapped my arm around her waist and circled her asshole with my middle and pointer fingers. Her back arched as she whimpered.

"Tell me what you want me to do," I commanded.

"Cum in me."

The rasp of her sweet tone was my undoing. I gave her just what she asked for. I released a low growl as I tried to control her movements, but she wasn't letting up. I let her use me for another orgasm before I laid her down and took control. Putting her legs by her ears, I filled her with deep, hard strokes that made it increasingly difficult to stay quiet. Each ooh and ahh, each whimper and hiss, each moan of my name... that shit drove me insane. We came again before I could even prepare.

"Shit," I moaned, rolling over so she could lay on top of me while I stayed inside of her.

"That was the start to a very good morning."

We chuckled as I rubbed her back. She kissed all over my face before laying her head on my chest and going right back to sleep.

Dauterive

Regina's eyes lit up as I placed the flowers and gift box on top of her desk. I appreciated how she'd been going above and beyond since the whole Trey situation arose and wanted to make sure I showed her that. Since she loved cashmere, I got her a sweater that I knew she'd wear and appreciate.

"Is this for me?" she asked, pulling the box forward.

"It is. Thank you for your commitment and dedication. I appreciate you more than you will ever know."

"You're so welcome, Doe. You know I love working with you. Now you get on out of here so you can go on your vacation. I got this."

"Yes, ma'am," I agreed before giving her a hug goodbye.

After our random lovemaking session this morning, Asylum and I got up and started planning. Our flight would leave at three this afternoon, and we were going to spend the rest of the week in Destin, Florida. I decided to drop Regina's gift off along with a few files I had at home after I finished packing. Asylum was running some last-minute errands, and since I was coming here and going straight home, I didn't bother calling Merc. In the time it would have taken him to meet me at home and trail me here, I could have come here and gotten back.

I didn't think too much about the impromptu trip and the dangers it could lead to until I got into my car and reversed, feeling an arm wrap around my neck. Hitting the brakes immediately, I yelped.

"Do you know how long I've been waiting to get you alone?" Trey asked in my ear before kissing it.

"Tr-Trey..."

"Drive the fuckin' car, Doe."

"And go where?"

"The place you should have never left... our home."

~

Asylum

As I WRAPPED up the last of my errands, I called Doe to see if she and True needed anything before I headed home. When she didn't answer, I called True. She answered quickly with, "Hello?"

"Hey, baby girl. Where's Doe?"

"Um... I'm not sure."

Looking back at Merc, I processed her words. "What do you mean? She's at the house, right?"

"No, sir. She left about an hour ago and said she'd be right back, but she hasn't come home yet."

"Did she say where she was going?" I asked, walking over to Merc.

"She said she was going to the office to drop some files

off and a gift for Mrs. Regina that was delivered earlier today."

"Shit. OK, baby. Thank you."

After disconnecting the call, I asked Merc, "Did Doe tell you she had to go somewhere today?"

His head shook as he pulled out his phone. "Nah. When I texted her this morning to see if anything was on the agenda she said no because y'all were going out of town. That's why I was so surprised when you pulled up."

Handing him my phone, I told him, "Let me see your phone so I can call Regina. While I do, track Doe's phone and car on mine."

"What's goin' on?" he asked, taking the phone.

"She's not at home and hasn't been for the past hour."

"Why in the fuck she ain't tell me she needed to go somewhere?" he asked with just as much confusion and frustration as I had, but I couldn't devote too much mental space to trying to figure that out. I'd ask her when I found her.

"I don't know, man," I said as I waited for Regina to answer.

"Dauterive Staffing, this is Regina. How may I help you?"

"Hey, Regina. Is Doe still there?"

"Asylum?" she confirmed. "No, she's not here. She left maybe thirty minutes ago."

"Did she say if she was going anywhere else?"

"She didn't. I told her to go home and get ready for her trip and she said OK."

"Aight. If you hear from her, let me know."

"Will do."

"Her location is at 40110 Sharp Square," Merc said as I pulled up the cameras that we'd installed at her office from his phone. Like mine, he would have to cut it on to get notifications, and because she wasn't supposed to be there today, he had the notifications off.

I watched as a male figure walked around her car. When he got in the back seat, I had to grip the phone tighter to keep from dropping it. I recognized the moment he made himself known because she immediately hit her brakes before carelessly swerving into traffic.

"He has her," I said, handing Merc his phone and grabbing mine.

"Then let's go get her."

～

Dauterive

I WATCHED as Trey paced back and forth. The amount of patience it took for him to wait for this moment unnerved me. I never thought I'd see the day where a man who claimed to love me would want to bring me so much harm. The longer I was in his presence, the more I regretted not calling Merc. Now, my impatience had put me in the same room as this crazy ass man, and I had no earthly idea what he was going to do.

He told me he'd been hiding out at one of his family's abandoned buildings from years ago. Every day, he'd been waiting and watching my every move when I went to work. Trey didn't follow me when I was with Asylum and Merc because he was confident if I went anywhere alone it would be my office.

I hated that he was right.

When I was no longer able to take the silence and

pacing, I asked, "What's your end goal, Trey? Why am I here?"

He hadn't tied me up or anything, and I was grateful for that, but he was holding a gun. I refamiliarized myself with the living room, taking in anything I could potentially use for a weapon. How the space was designed, I had more of a chance fighting him than trying to just run out. The front door was too far away for me to risk him catching me. I'd have to at least wound him before I made a run for it.

"You're here because this is where you belong." He stopped pacing and looked at me. "I've been waiting for you to come to your senses about that, but it's obviously not going to happen."

"Trey." My tone was just as tired as I was of this back and forth. He was fighting harder to get me back than he was to make me happy while he had me... which made absolutely no sense. "You have a whole baby with someone else."

"Ah ah ah." He wiggled his pointer finger. "My baby mama will not be a problem. If she's the reason you don't want to be with me anymore, I'll kill her, and we can raise the baby as if he was our own."

That statement made me realize just how unstable he truly was. The fact that he was willing to kill an innocent woman just to be with me told me he'd do the same to Asylum if he had the chance. I'd watched enough thrillers and Lifetime movies to know going against him would only lead to him being violent. Instead, I decided to pacify him and make him believe what he wanted was possible until Asylum came for me. Because he would come for me. There was no doubt in my mind about that.

"No you don't... you don't have to do that, Trey. That baby will need his mother and..."

"You can be TJ's mother. That's what I'm saying. That's how it should have been all along."

Nodding, I swallowed hard. "Trey, I appreciate all that you've done to get me back, but I've rebuilt my life without you. You made me feel really unsafe and I don't think I can trust you anymore. Look at you now. You kidnapped me and you have a gun. How am I supposed to come back to a man like that?"

He looked down at the gun in his hand as if he'd forgotten he was even holding it.

"I can't believe you would say that, love. You know you've *always* been safe with me."

"Have I?" I scoffed. "You had me drugged and set my house on fire. You broke into my parents' home and tried to kill me..."

"I was upset!" he roared, causing me to jump. "You chose that nigga over me! You didn't even give me a chance to fix things between us. It's me or nobody, Doe. You either gon' be with me, or you die. Which one do you choose?"

Cupping my hands in my lap, I inhaled a deep breath as my heart raced. "If you can prove that I can trust you to never cheat again and that I'll be safe with you, I'll come back to you."

"How do I prove that?" he asked, kneeling in front of me.

"First, you have to put the gun away." Trey's head immediately began to shake. "How do you expect me to trust you if you don't trust me?"

He thought about it for a few seconds before standing and pulling me up with him. "OK, but if you try anything, I will kill you, Dauterive."

Nodding my agreement, I prayed silently. We walked

into what used to be our bedroom, where he put the gun back in his closet safe.

"Thank you," I mumbled.

"Now what?"

"Is the baby here?"

His head tilted and he eyed my frame. "He is. Why?"

"Where is his mother, Trey?"

"She's at work."

"We need to take the baby to her. I don't want any distractions when we start to rekindle our bond." My fingers trembled as I placed my hands on his chest and rubbed it. The moment he gripped my waist and pulled me closer, vomit threatened to erupt from my throat. I swallowed it down quickly, willing myself not to show how I truly felt about having his arms around me.

"You mean that?" The innocence in his tone made my eyes water. Nibbling my cheek, I blinked rapidly, trying to search his eyes for what had gone wrong inside his mind when I tried to leave his heart. This wasn't merely a narcissist trying to reclaim what he believed was his. Trey had some serious mental issues going on right now, and I couldn't help but wonder how long they had been bubbling and trying to get to the surface before now.

"I mean it, love. Go get the baby and we can take him to his mom. Then, we can focus on us."

"OK, but if you try anything..."

"You'll kill me, I know."

Rolling my eyes, I removed myself from his grip.

We walked to the baby's room, where TJ was sleeping peacefully. "Did you leave him by himself to come get me?"

"Yes, but I'd just put him down to sleep and knew I wouldn't be gone long. Today is the first day I came back home and his mama couldn't wait until later for us to spend some time together."

Nodding, I followed him out of the room as he carried the baby out in his car seat. "Do you need me to grab anything for him?"

He looked back at me with a smile. "Nah. I keep a to-go bag for him by the door."

"That's smart," I complimented, hoping it would soften him even more.

Once we were outside, I waited until he was busy putting the car seat in the back seat to take off running. At the top of my lungs, I screamed for help, hoping someone would hear me and open their door. Worst case scenario, he'd chase after me. Without the gun, I wasn't in as much fear.

I made it halfway down the street before I saw a couple sitting on their front porch. At the sight of me, they stood.

"Hel—argh!"

Trey tackled me from behind. He flipped me over and began to choke me. I dug my thumbs into his eyes until he released my neck. Standing, I tried to run again, but he grabbed my ankle and pulled, forcing me to fall onto my stomach.

"Hey!" the older white man yelled from his porch. "Get off her! We're calling the cops!"

His threat didn't seem to register in Trey's mind. He flipped me over and held my arms down with his knees.

"I told you if I can't have you no one can," he taunted, choking me again. "You thought this shit was a game, huh?"

No matter how much I wiggled and fought underneath him, I couldn't move. I looked into his eyes as mine watered, and they were so dark and lifeless. It became harder and harder to breathe as tears fell from my eyes. Just as I finally began to give up, the sound of tires screeching filled my ears. My eyes fluttered as I felt myself become lightheaded.

A loud popping sound rang out, sending a bullet through Trey's forehead. He fell back onto my legs, releasing the hold he had around my throat instantly.

As I coughed, I tried to kick him off me. A hand gripped my arm and lifted me from the street. Dropping the gun, Asylum cupped my cheeks as he looked me over intently.

"Are you hurt?" he checked.

My mouth opened and closed but nothing would come out. I burst into tears, and he pulled me into his arms. Hugging his neck tightly, I squeezed my eyes shut as the weight of what had happened finally settled within me.

My ex-husband was about to kill me.

My ex-husband was dead.

Asylum

L ater that Night

TRUE WAS CUDDLED up on Doe sleeping peacefully. What started as her comforting Dauterive turned into her snoring like a grown ass man. I knew how deep Doe was in her thoughts when the sound didn't faze her. She gripped her mug of tea tightly as she stared into the distance. With Doe's account and two eyewitness statements, me killing Trey was considered defense of others. No charges would be brought against me. His son was taken to his mother, and unless Doe was included in his will or something, she would never have to see or worry about him again.

I picked True up to carry her to bed and Doe looked up at me with a smile. Once I had True settled, I made my way back to the living room. Doe took a sip of her tea as I sat next to her.

"You wanna talk about it?"

Her head shook. "There's really nothing to talk about.

He was going to kill me if you hadn't shown up." She took my hand into hers. "This makes twice that you saved my life."

"I'm concerned about how seeing that is going to affect you," I admitted. I for damn sure wouldn't lose any sleep over putting a bullet between his eyes, but I was worried about Doe. No matter how crazy he was acting, Trey was still a man she had a lot of love for at one point. I couldn't imagine how traumatizing today was for her.

"His eyes were lifeless long before you killed him. That's what I keep seeing. His eyes. How he stared down at me as he choked me." Absently, her hand went to her bruised neck. "I'm sure it'll take some time for me to stop seeing that. But I'm... I'm OK. I hate he had to die but I'm glad this nightmare is over." She straddled me. "I don't want you worried about me. I'll be OK. If I feel like I can't handle it on my own, I'll talk to a professional. I promise."

That eased my nerves a little. I gripped her waist and gently rocked her against me as I asked, "Why didn't you call Merc, Dauterive?"

She smiled and hung her head. "It was supposed to be a quick trip. I didn't want to inconvenience him."

"Outside of Haley, he's my best friend and that's literally what I was paying him for, sweetheart."

"I know, I know," she whined. "I guess I got a bit too relaxed because Trey hadn't been reaching out. But you know what? I'm glad I did because it's finally over."

That was true. I was cool with waiting for him to slip up, but I knew having a guard wasn't something she wanted to deal with for a long period of time.

"What's most important is that it's finally over and he won't be able to hurt you again."

"Thanks to you," she cooed, leaning forward to kiss me.

Our tongues slowly swirled around each other as I held her close. I'd been thanking God all day for allowing me to find and save her. I didn't believe He'd bring her back into my world just to take her in such a permanent way.

THAT WEEKEND

THOUGH I INSISTED it wasn't necessary, Doe's parents wanted to do something to show me their appreciation. They hired a private chef for us, who decorated the living room and set us up for a romantic dinner date. When dinner was over, they stopped by briefly to give me gifts I really didn't want to accept. What I did for Doe wasn't something that needed to be rewarded, though I appreciated the gesture.

"We know how much you love skiing and snow, so we hope you enjoy the trip and the other things we got you," Drew said with a wide grin.

They'd booked me a suite at a resort and spa in Denver along with pre-paying for every adventure and activity I could think of to do while I was there.

"I appreciate y'all, but y'all really didn't have to do all that you did."

"We wanted to thank you physically for what you did, son," Hamilton said. "Dauterive's life is priceless, but these gifts are just a way to show you a bit of our appreciation."

"I can respect that, so I accept. Thank you both."

They both gave me hugs before hugging Doe and heading out. We might not have been able to go to Florida, but this gave me another trip to look forward to after Christmas.

"This was very nice of them," Doe said, taking a sip of her wine.

The chef had retired for the evening, leaving behind a moist white cake topped with buttercream icing and strawberries that I was tempted to eat off my woman.

"Yeah, I love how your parents love you."

"They love you too. Even without knowing where our relationship was going to go when we first came back into each other's lives, they were accepting you back as their son."

I chuckled because that was true. That was further confirmation that what Doe and I shared was real. My folks loved her, and her folks loved me. Back then, they rooted for us to get our shit together. And now, they were happy we were getting back to us.

"You're right. I'm just glad things are returning to normal again," I said as I sat down next to her on the thick blanket the chef set up.

"Speaking of which... How are we going to do Christmas? It's a week away."

"What you wanna do? I got the two best gifts in the world already."

Doe blushed as she wrapped her arm around mine and rested her head on my shoulder. "I want us to start our own tradition," she suggested. "We do Friendsgiving with the crew and Christmas Eve."

"That's true."

"So maybe we can do a Christmas breakfast with our families here then do something else with just me, you, and True."

"I'm with that. Christmas really don't hit the same no more. Once True opens her gifts and starts playing with them I be over it."

She laughed. "OK, let's think of something we can do to stay in the Christmas spirit."

We thought about it silently for a while before an idea came to me. "Aight, so how about we do a little volunteer work on Christmas Eve before kicking it with the crew. Christmas morning, we can have our families over for breakfast like you suggested, then go to church together. After that, you and I can have the afternoon to do whatever we want alone while True indulges in her gifts. And that evening, we can make cookies and drink eggnog while watching Christmas movies one last time with her."

Doe gave me a kiss on the cheek. "That sounds absolutely perfect! I love that."

Our conversation shifted as we began to feed each other the cake. Before I knew it, two hours had passed of us talking and chilling on the living room floor. I knew there was more to life and fancier or more extravagant ways to be with the one you loved, but I was convinced Doe and I had the most fun and deepened our bond during moments like this.

Dauterive

The Weekend After Christmas

WE DECIDED to take True to Destin before we went to Denver. Since we worked for ourselves, it was easy to make the accommodations. I had to admit, having my own little family made me want to work less and be with them more. Asylum loving to travel as much as I did was truly like the icing on the cake.

True and I had gotten closer now that she'd been back home. I think our bond was so great because it was a true friendship. At first, I felt weird trying to be a pre-teen's friend, but I believed it humanized her in my eyes. She wasn't just my man's kid. She was a human being with thoughts, feelings, goals, and desires. I loved the time we spent together and how easy it was for us to get along.

"Ms. Doe," True called as I packed the last of my things in my carryon bag.

"Wassup, True?"

"When are you going to decorate your she-shed?"

I paused for a moment to look at her through the mirror. She had a breakdown when Sy cleared her mother's things from the she-shed and now she was appearing to be ready for me to replace them with mine.

"I'm not sure, baby love."

"Why not?"

"Well... I know that was your mom's space. Even though they are now divorced, I never wanted you to think I was trying to take her place. Plus, I technically don't live here." I laughed. "Now that my little situation has been handled, I can leave and move to my own place at any time."

She frowned. "Why would you leave us?"

The question was simple, but I didn't have an answer for her.

Why would I leave them?

I was already calling this my home and Sy my man, though neither of those things had been made official yet.

"Daddy!" she called, taking my silence as her chance to bring Sy into the conversation.

It wasn't long before he was bringing his fine ass into the bathroom. This was truly one man I'd never be able to get enough of. And every time I saw the tattoo of my face on his neck I smiled because he couldn't get enough of me either. Not even time and distance had been able to tear us apart.

"What y'all in here planning?" he asked, already knowing we were quick to double team him into doing something, though it often wasn't necessary because he spoiled us both.

"Ms. Doe said she's going to leave us."

He scowled immediately as she wrapped her arm around him, looking at me with a smile.

"I didn't say I was going to leave," I clarified through my laugh. "I said because I don't live here, and that situation is over, I can leave at any time."

"Why would you leave us?" he asked, and even though they weren't related by blood, they both were looking at me with the same confused expression.

I couldn't help but laugh as I looked from one to the other.

"You haven't asked her to stay," True said.

"You haven't even asked me to be your girlfriend."

"Oh." His head bobbed as realization covered his face. "I see where the confusion is stemming from." Asylum closed the space between us, pushing my hair out of my face and onto my back. "Why would I ask you to be my girlfriend when we both know you're going to be my wife?" My mouth opened and closed but no words came out. "And why would I ask you to stay when you know this is where you belong?"

"Well..." My voice grew quiet as I considered his questions. "I might think those things, but I want you to validate them for me so I will know."

"I'm gonna go before y'all get nasty," True said, making us both laugh.

Asylum waited until we were alone to say, "That's fair." He placed me on the counter, so we were eye to eye. "I love you, and I would be honored if we could go back to where we were before we took our break."

"Wait, do you mean literally where we were or..."

"I do." Lifting my hand, he kissed it. "I want us to be engaged again. Is that OK with you?"

For a second I couldn't speak. I knew our bond was still

the same if not even deeper now. Hearing him express he felt and wanted the same things as I did hit my heart in a place that hadn't been touched in thirteen years.

"That's OK with me," I replied with a grin.

"Good. And this is your home, so yo' ass ain't goin' nowhere. You can decorate it however you'd like to make it feel like yours... because it is yours."

With a nod, I wrapped my arms around his neck and kissed his lips. I didn't think anything could make spending the weekend with my babies better but having this clarity on our relationship did.

Asylum

As happy as I was about spending time with Doe and True in Florida, I didn't think anything would ruin my mood until I noticed all the missed calls from Selena and Bobby. When I was on vacation, I kept my phone on Do Not Disturb. Those that were closest to me knew to reach me they would have to call because those on my favorite's list would automatically come through. They only called if it was an actual emergency though.

After bringing everyone's bags in, we all pretty much went our separate ways. I went to my man cave so I could return Bobby's calls. I figured Selena was calling on his behalf, so I decided to reach out to her later. When he responded, loud music and wind blowing could be heard in the background. He turned it down then spoke.

"You act like you don't have my child with you. I need to be able to get in touch with you at all times. Ain't no reason for my calls to be ignored."

I laughed like this nigga was a real-life comedian. "And

you act like it don't take me but one hit to knock yo' ass out for disrespect. Watch how the fuck you talk to me, Bobby."

He exhaled hard. "Look, I didn't call you to argue."

"I wasn't gon' argue with you anyway, but what do you want?"

"I'ma be real with you. I wanted True back for a reason." I knew that, but I remained silent so he could continue. "My old man is sick, and you know he's one of the main ones that felt like I should have been doing more for True." I nodded my agreement. "He really been on one since I got with a woman that had kids. He's threatening to take me out his will if I don't do right by my child. That's why I wanted her to come live with me."

Laughing, I reached for the brown box in the center of the coffee table for a blunt. I wish I had him on speaker-phone for Doe to hear because she wasn't going to believe this shit.

"Now if you try to take her away from me, I'ma lose out on this money. If you drop the case, I'll cut you in on my profit after my daddy die. Then, you can have her back."

Squeezing the bridge of my nose, I tried to decide what racing thought I wanted to reply with. This nigga really just said he wanted custody of his child for a life insurance payout. *The fuck?*

"So let me get this straight." I laughed again as I began to pace. "You want me to let True live with you until your father dies so you can get some insurance money from his will?"

"Yep," he said confidently.

"How much will you get, Bobby?"

"Quarter of a mil."

"Quarter of a... That's all True is worth to you?" When

he didn't respond, I added, "I'll double that shit if you sign over your rights and stay the fuck away from my daughter."

Silence filled the line before he stuttered, "D-d-double? Y-you gon' g-give me d-double?"

"Ain't that what I said?"

"Five hundred thousand dollars just to give up my rights?" He chuckled. "Tell me where to sign."

The happiness that I wanted to consume me didn't. Not immediately. My first emotion was sadness. Sadness over the fact that he could give her up so easily. Then I felt anger. Anger over the fact that God blessed him with a daughter to begin with. Then I felt relieved. Relieved over the fact that she would never have to deal with this man again. And as I accepted his words, that happiness consumed me.

"Aight, Bobby. I'll text you a time and address to meet me at my attorney's office so we can get this taken care of."

"Cool. And don't be bullshittin' me, man. That money gon' change me and my girl's life."

My eyes rolled to the ceiling as I shook my head. "I'll hit you up."

I quickly disconnected the call, ready to be done with his ass. I texted True and told her to meet me outside, then sent Doe a text telling her the same. They arrived at the same time. I looked out into nature as I took a few pulls from my blunt. Usually I didn't smoke around True, but since we were outside, I didn't mind. Plus, the shit with Bobby had really just blown my mind. I'd never been so appreciative yet angry with a person at the same time.

"Is everything OK?" Doe asked.

"Yeah, uh..." I looked at True, and the innocence of her expression made me care less about my feelings for Bobby and more about the fact that my girl would finally be mine. "I just got off the phone with Bobby and..."

True's eyes rolled as she crossed her arms over her chest. "He's not trying to take me back, is he?"

To spare her the details, I said, "The opposite. He's going to let you live with me full time if that's what you want."

"Wait, how?" Doe asked.

"We can talk about that later," I told her. "But to make the story short, he's agreed to sign over his rights." I gave True my attention. "If that's what you want."

"What would that mean?"

"It would mean he would no longer legally be considered your father. You won't have to go live with him ever, and he won't have a say in your life."

"Does that mean you'll be my legal daddy?"

Smiling, I shook my head. "Not legally. I'll have my attorney include that he's making me your guardian while your mom is away, but technically, the only way I'll legally be your dad is if I adopted you."

True looked from me to Doe. When her eyes returned to mine, she took a small step in my direction and asked, "Can you? Can you adopt me?"

Even though that was what I'd always wanted to do, there was something about her asking me to do it that caught me off guard. All I could do was stare at her as I swallowed back my tears. Doe rubbed my back softly, keeping me steady as she always did.

My stabilizer.

And my baby girl.

Clearing my throat, I ran my hand down my neck and tried to keep my tears from falling. "I'm truly honored that you would want me to be your legal dad, True. You don't have to do that if you don't really want to, though. You know I love you as if you were my own and I'll take care of you for as long as I need to."

She smiled and shook her head. "I know that, but I want to. You've always been my daddy. I love you."

That made it impossible for me to hold in my tears. I was an expressive man, but I wasn't overly emotional, and I never cried. Anything concerning this little girl, though, could bring tears to my eyes. I pulled her in for a hug as I told her, "Then I would love to. But we would have to wait until your mom came back. It would be a big mess if we tried to do this without her consent."

Unless her parents had her declared dead because she'd been missing now for over two months, she was still technically True's primary guardian. Bobby would be able to sign over his rights, but I wouldn't be able to have any instated without her consent.

"Ugh, she ruins *everything*!" True almost yelled as she pulled away from me. "That's my mama and I love her, but I'm so angry that she left us! And now she's *still* messing things up!"

As she stomped away, I resisted the urge to follow her. True was the kind of child who needed time to process things on her own before she listened to what anyone had to say. I'd check on her in about an hour or so.

"Poor baby," Doe said, wrapping her arms around herself.

"I had no desire to try and find Sierra again until now."

"Yeah. I mean, if there was ever a reason for her to bring her ass home, this would be it."

"You know that mane agreed to give up his rights for half a million dollars?"

"Are you serious?" Doe asked, taking the blunt from me

that I'd completely forgotten about after True asked what she asked.

I told her the entire story, and she was just as blown away as I was. I wouldn't question it, though. If he was willing to give True to me for that check, I'd have my attorney draw up an agreement first thing in the morning.

Dauterive

M id-January

Life was good.

Bobby had, in fact, signed over his rights to True.

We still hadn't heard from Sierra, but I was just glad Bobby was out of the way along with Trey.

I had returned to a sense of normalcy with work and was working on securing a contract with a Fortune 500 Company that would allow me to staff them for the next five years. There were still moments where I had flashbacks about what happened with Trey, but I was just so grateful that he was out of my life that I didn't dwell on them for too long.

Tonight, True was going to be spending the evening with Grandma Yvonne and Grandpa Vernon. Haley and Antonne were having an event that Sy and I couldn't miss. They requested we wear all white, so I chose a form fitting, floor-length, long-sleeved dress that I paired with silver accessories. Usually I would go with gold but Asylum favored silver and platinum. With his white tuxedo, he accessorized it with diamond studs, his platinum diamond grill, and a silver chain and Rolex. I admired him as he slid a platinum diamond ring onto his pinky finger. God put an extra helping of sexy into this man... *damn*!

"C'mere," he requested, looking at me through the mirror.

I made my way over to him, and he wrapped his arms around me. The kisses he placed on my neck had my pussy leaking as I released a quiet moan.

"If you don't stop, we're going to be late."

"You're worth it." He looked at us in the mirror and said, "We look so good together."

"I agree."

"I have the most beautiful woman in the world. Damn." I blushed as he kissed my cheek. "You know what I love most, though?" he asked, turning me to face him.

"What?"

"How well we complement each other spiritually, mentally, and emotionally—not just physically. I've never had a person feel like they were literally my other half besides you. God taught me what it means to have a rib with you." He kissed the palms of my hands. "I protect so many people, but you protect my heart. You're my stabilizer and I will spend the rest of my days trying to make your life as happy and peaceful as you've made mine and True's."

I wasn't expecting him to get that deep, and his declaration brought tears to my eyes. Now I wanted to leave even less. As I began to unbutton his pants, Asylum gripped my hands and laughed.

"What you doin'?"

"About to make love to my man."

"We can later, I promise. We really have to go so we won't be late."

"OK, but I love you, Asylum. I respect you. I appreciate you. I support you. And I'm genuinely just so happy to have you and True. You're one of one, and I am blessed to be able to experience you now and forever... always in all ways."

"Mm," he moaned, biting down on his bottom lip. "You think you slick, huh?"

"What do you mean?" I asked with a giggle. He lowered my hand to his hardening dick.

"You know what talking that talk does to me."

"And you know what this does to me." I gripped his shaft through his pants. "But you're right. We really have to go."

As I walked past him, he smacked my ass before picking me up and carrying me out of the bathroom as I laughed.

EXCITEMENT SIZZLED up my spine as Sy and I walked into the event center hand in hand. We'd just finished hanging up our coats, and I couldn't wait to see what Haley and Antonne had come up with tonight. When we stepped inside, the music that was originally playing stopped, and all eyes were on us.

Everyone else in the room had on black and for a moment I thought I was losing my mind.

"Babe," I called quietly as we walked toward the crowd.

"Hmm?"

"Didn't the invitation say wear white?"

He chuckled. "Yeah, it did."

"Then why is everyone else in black?"

As I scanned the faces of the crowd, my steps halted

when I noticed my parents and sister along with Asylum's grandparents and True.

"Sy..."

He looked at me with a soft smile. "Yeah, sweetheart?"

"What's going on?"

He walked me closer to the crowd—close enough for them to hear us but far enough away for it to feel like we still had privacy.

"I wanted to do this right."

He went into his pocket and pulled out a blush pink halo pear-shaped diamond ring that made my mouth water. Chuckling, I stepped back with a shake of my head. I knew he would get me a ring eventually, but I wasn't expecting him to do all this. What most blew me away was the size of the ring. It was three or four times bigger than the one he was able to afford when he first proposed.

Asylum never shied away from sharing with me how he was financially stable enough to take care of me and seeing as he dropped half a million in less than twenty-four hours, that was proof of his wealth but still. The ring looked to be at least five carats, and I wasn't expecting something so beautiful and extravagant.

As he slipped the ring on my finger, he said, "I'd like to believe thirteen years ago, like Adam, I needed time to get myself together to be worthy of you. It may have taken us a while to get to this point, but you have become the apex of God's creations to me. I slept, waiting for this moment for all those years, and now that you're back in my life... I'm finally awake. Like I told you at home, you're my rib. This ring and our commitment to each other will represent your return to where you belong." As I clutched mine, Sy placed my hand in the center of his chest... On his heart. I closed my eyes as tears fell at the revelation that our hearts were beating in sync. "Will you mar—"

"Yes!" I yelled, making him laugh as he licked his lips. "My answer to you will always be yes, Sy. Yes!"

As we embraced, everyone around us cheered. I tuned them out and lost myself in his arms.

"I love you," he muttered against my lips before kissing them.

"I love you too." Giggling, I looked at the ring. "Are we really doing this?"

"We are, and this is literally just the beginning."

My arms wrapped around him again, and his lips returned to mine. This was the best way to start the new year.

Asylum

T wo Weeks Later

I'd been out shopping for gifts to get my girls for Valentine's Day when I came home and got the surprise of my life. Sierra was at the gate waiting for me. When I questioned why the guards didn't call to let me know she was here, she said she wanted me to be surprised.

For quite some time, I envisioned how this moment would play out in my head. As I stared at her, none of the things I thought I would say came out. None of the things I thought I would feel were at the surface. I wasn't happy because I loved her and she was safe nor was I angry that she'd left and just now returned. I was completely indifferent, and for a man like me, that was the worst state for a woman like her to have me in.

"Are those gifts for True?" she asked, peeping into my car. "Looks like there's more than last year. And you've started what... two weeks early?"

"These are for True and my fiancée. And yeah, I'm getting started early. I'm taking my fiancée on a trip for the week of Valentine's Day, so we're celebrating with True next week."

Her eyes blinked rapidly as she tried to process my words. It was like a circuit was shorting in her brain and she couldn't wrap her mind around what she'd just heard. She kept opening and closing her mouth, but nothing came out. When it no longer amused me, I told Blake, "She's no longer welcome here. If she stops by, call me immediately and do not let her in."

"Asylum... wait... I..."

Rolling up the window, I ignored her as I drove inside the gate. Her ass had been gone for four months and wanted to make small talk like it had been four minutes. By the time I'd parked in the garage Sierra was calling me. Apparently, she'd gotten a new phone with the same number. Had I thought she would do that, I would've blocked her shit. Still, I answered... only because she was True's mother.

"What?"

"We need to talk."

"You haven't wanted to talk for the last four months, so I don't really care about what you have to say now."

She sighed. "Regardless of how you feel, my daughter is in your home and..."

"Oh, *now* you give a fuck about your daughter?" I laughed and shook my head. "You wasn't thinking about True when you abandoned her. She good, SiSi. Now get off my property before I have you escorted off."

"Sy, please!" she yelled, and I could hear her composure breaking. "I'm sorry, OK? If you'd just give me two minutes, I'll leave."

"You got two minutes, and that's including the time it'll take you to get down here."

"Asylum, I…"

I hung up the phone and got out of the car. As I got out, I saw her running down the driveway because her car was parked on the opposite side of the gate. Crossing my ankles, I leaned against the trunk and chuckled. At least she was serious about having this conversation.

When she made her way in front of me, she palmed her knees as she gasped for air.

"You're down to a minute, Sierra."

"Wa-wait." She held up her finger as she took in a deep breath. Standing upright, she looked into my eyes as she said, "I hate you, Sy."

"I'd say so. You did leave me with no conversation."

"Like you cared. You made it clear you were only going to stay with me because of my daughter."

"And? That's the same daughter you lied to me about, costing me the love of my life. You lucky I didn't say worse."

She rolled her eyes and crossed her arms over her heaving chest. "Look… I'm not going to apologize for what I did to you. I was upset and I wanted to hurt you. I knew there was nothing I could do to hurt you the way hearing you say that hurt me. So… I did the one thing I knew would trigger you. I left True."

I knew there was a deeper reason behind her disappearance, but I wasn't expecting it to be that. As unbothered as I was when I first saw her, hearing her say that pissed me off. She didn't just intentionally do something that she knew would hurt me, but she hurt her daughter in the process to trigger me.

"True was innocent in this, and you used her because you knew that was the only way you could get to me. I shared with you what my mother did to me in confidence, and the moment you had to pay for your fucked up lie you decided to use that shit against me? Do you realize what you've done to your daughter just to make me feel something for your ass?"

"I'm sorry!" she wailed as her tears started to fall. "You wouldn't love me, so I settled for hate! But I... I wasn't thinking clearly about the damage it would do to True. By the time I realized it, I was too ashamed to come back. I've just now gathered the courage to face her." Sierra chuckled as she wiped her eyes. "And here you are engaged already. It took you less than six months to replace me. You really didn't give a fuck about me, did you?"

"I didn't replace you; you were a replacement for a woman who was irreplaceable. And with you finally out of the way, she's back where she rightfully belongs." My confession had her stunned and speechless. "I want you off my property. Now."

It wasn't until I gently pushed her out of the garage so I could close it, that she said, "Fine. Send True out and we'll leave."

I laughed. "True ain't going no-fucking-where."

Scoffing, she put her hands on her hips. "That's my child. I can take her wherever I damn well please."

I rubbed my palms together as I closed the distance between us. "A lot has changed since you've been gone, SiSi. Bobby signed over his rights to True. With his permission, and signed off on by a judge, I am True's temporary primary guardian. Before you can get her, you'll need to not only prove you're mentally well and financially stable, but that you have a stable, safe living environment for her to come to that will not disrupt the normal routine we've created for her here. Once you've done that, you can call me. Until then, stay the fuck away from my house and *my* daughter."

The roar she released turned into a cry as her small fists began to fly like windmills. I grabbed them and held them at her sides as I turned her around and pulled her into my chest. My guards wasted no time running toward us. Before they arrived to escort her off my land, I whispered in her ear, "My mama had to learn the hard way what happens when you fuck with me. Now, you're going to learn too."

~

A FEW HOURS Later

"YOU'RE DOING THE RIGHT THING," Doe said, squeezing my hand gently.

Now that I'd calmed down some, I accepted that I needed to let True know her mom was back ASAP. Whether Sierra's actions were wrong or not, I wouldn't keep her away from True... especially if True wanted to see her. True had gotten to a place where she didn't even ask about her mother anymore. I still asked her how she was feeling about everything at least twice a week to check on her mental and emotional wellbeing.

Her stance was the same—she loved her mom, missed her, and hoped she was OK—but she hated that Sierra had left us. I loved that True genuinely cared about me. She wasn't just mad about her loss; she considered mine too. Even though she knew I didn't love her mother the way a husband should, she knew about what happened during my childhood and how seeing her experience the same thing hurt me.

"I know that in my heart, but my mind is telling me to protect her from Sierra's bullshit. She's back now, but there's no guarantee she's going to stay. As upset as she was, what if she leaves again?"

"Unfortunately, we can't say, babe. Even if she does leave again, True deserves to know the truth. I know it's second nature for you to protect her, but if she finds out Sierra is back and that you didn't tell her, I don't want you to have to deal with her not trusting you as much."

That possibility was the main reason I decided to tell her today. The last thing I needed was for Sierra to have Selena call True and give her the news. Since she was escorted off my property, Sierra hadn't reached back out. Depending on what True wanted, that would determine my next move.

"You're right. Let's just get this over with."

We headed to True's room, where she was watching a series on Netflix about sea animals. The shit was weird, but she loved it and I loved that she loved to learn. She smiled at the sight of us as she sat up in bed.

"Are we about to go out to eat?"

I chuckled with a shake of my head. She was just as bad as Doe when it came to getting tired of healthy meal prep. After what I had to tell her, she could get just about whatever she wanted from me.

"If you want to. But there's something your daddy has to tell you first," Doe said, gently pushing me closer to her bed.

I sat on the edge of it and ran my hand down my face. "Your mom is back."

I waited and watched her reaction. It didn't change.

"Oh. That's good."

Doe and I looked at each other. "Yeah, she stopped by earlier."

True nodded. "Is she staying? I don't want to get happy and she start seeing me just a couple of times like my daddy."

That shit broke my heart. I swallowed the frustration brewing within me, hating that SiSi's actions had now made it difficult for True to trust her. That trust provided safety in relationships that would go far beyond their mother-daughter one. If I didn't make sure she maintained a healthy perspective of this and healed her mother wound as early as possible, there was no telling how toxic True's friendships and romantic relationships would be.

"Honestly, I don't know, baby girl. She does want to see you. Do you want to see her? Maybe you can ask her that yourself."

"I'll see her, but not right now. You taught me if I don't have anything nice to say, don't say anything at all. I'm too mad at her right now, but I am happy she's back."

"Take all the time you need, True."

I gave her a hug and asked if she still wanted to go grab something to eat. She said she no longer had an appetite. Doe asked her if she wanted to hang with us and she said she'd rather be alone. I'd give her space to process how she was feeling like I always did. Hopefully she'd return to her normal self soon, otherwise, that was going to be another thing for me to hold against Sierra.

∾

ONE WEEK Later

. . .

185

IT TOOK True four days to decide she was ready to see her mother. When she was, I called Sierra and made plans for them to meet. We chose the neutral location of her parents' home. Even though I was in the kitchen with them, I gave True my word that I wouldn't say anything unless she wanted me to. Leaning against the sink, I watched as they stared at each other. She didn't even hug SiSi when we first arrived, and I honestly didn't know how this meeting would end.

"Daddy said you left to hurt him," was the first thing True said.

Sierra's brows wrinkled as she shook her head. "Bobby had nothing to do with this."

"I'm not talking about him. I'm talking about *him*," she replied, pointing at me.

"Since when did you stop calling him Daddy Sy?"

"Since you left me, and my other daddy did a horrible job taking care of me. He didn't talk to me, play with me, *or* care for me. He didn't pray for me or take me to school. He didn't do any of the things Sy does for me. So I decided if anyone should be my daddy it was him." She paused before adding, "I want him to adopt me. Can he?"

Sierra's mouth hung open as her head shook. "True, I... I didn't come here to talk to you about that. I mean... Sy and I have always discussed that happening, but I want to talk about us."

True's head tilted as she cupped her hands on top of the table. "OK. What?"

Sierra swallowed hard. "I wanted to apologize. I did leave you because I was upset with Sy. I didn't think about how that would affect you fully. I should have taken you with me."

"I'm glad you didn't."

Covering my mouth as I suppressed my smile, I shook my head.

"Wow. If you're talking like this after four months of being with him, I don't think I want to allow him to adopt you."

True sighed as she straightened her posture. "I'm talking like this because I hate what you did. I love you, but I don't like you very much right now." She paused, and I wondered if she was finally about to break. "You left me!" she yelled, tears finally starting to fall. "How could you do that to me!" I wanted to comfort her, but I let Sierra wrap her in an embrace. Even though True clung to her, she still let her have it. "You said you loved me but that was a lie! You don't do that to people you love!"

"I do love you, baby, I swear," Sierra said as her tears fell. "That's why I left you with Asylum. I knew he would take care of you while I was gone." Sierra kneeled in front of True and wiped her tears. "Mommy was sick in her head *and* her heart. I wasn't thinking clearly with either one. I was obsessed with earning your daddy's love when it should have been freely given. I know that now, and I'm in a much better place mentally and emotionally. I know you might not believe me, but I want to show you." Sierra looked over at me. "We can take it as slow as you want. I'll even let you continue to stay with Sy until you're comfortable living with me."

Her head shook adamantly. "I don't want to stay with just you. Not all the time. And I want him to adopt me."

"OK, OK," Sierra conceded. "You can stay with him until you're comfortable trusting I will never do anything like this again. Then, we can work out some kind of living arrangement. Maybe you can stay with him two weeks and me two weeks out of the month. How does that sound?"

True looked back at me. I didn't want to influence her decision, so I told her, "It's on you, baby girl."

She thought it over before saying, "OK. I would like that. Can he adopt me?"

Sierra chuckled as she eyed me with more tears falling from hers. "Of course he can adopt you. There's no one I trust with you more than him." Standing, she made her way in front of me. "I'm sorry for destroying us. And for lying to you. I knew even back then that you were a great man and I wanted you. A part of me felt like if I had time to prove that I was a great woman you'd love me the way I was falling in love with you. I was wrong for lying about True then and I was wrong for leaving the both of you now. Will you ever be able to forgive me?"

I wanted to tell her no, but like with my mother, that forgiveness that she thought she needed wasn't for her; it was for me. Apologizing may have dissolved her of her guilt but forgiving her was going to be the only thing to dissolve my anger.

"Eventually," I admitted honestly. "Right now, we'll be at peace just as long as you do right by True. The minute you show me you won't be consistent and hurt her again, I'm going to do everything in my power to fully take her away from you."

Sierra nodded as she told me, "Trust me... it won't come to that."

I nodded and headed to the living room so they could continue to talk. By the time we all agreed to part ways, we came to the agreement that True would spend weekends with Sierra here until she got a job and her own place. Then, we'd allow her to spend half the month at both of our homes.

Next week, Sierra and Doe would need to get

acquainted again so she'd see the woman that had been helping keep both me and True sane. As long as Sierra didn't exhibit any signs of possession over us toward Doe, I felt like we'd all be good. But I meant what I said, if I felt like I couldn't trust True with her, I'd get rid of her just like I'd gotten rid of Bobby.

Dauterive

Two Weeks Later

As Asylum and I made ourselves comfortable in our first-class seats, I couldn't wipe the smile from my face. He was taking me to one of my favorite islands for Valentine's Day —Turks and Caicos. True was going to be spending the week at her grandparents' house with Sierra, and I was glad they'd be able to spend some extra time together.

So far, the arrangement was going well. Because Sierra was working weekdays, she was grateful to have her for the weekends and picked her up on Fridays after school, and she also took her to school on Mondays. We met last weekend, and it was cordial. I didn't see us being friends any time soon, but we had a mutual respect because of the people we loved. I made it clear to her that I wasn't trying to take her place with True; I was simply an extra person to love her. I also made it clear to her that I wouldn't be dealing with that baby mama drama bullshit she pulled all those years ago. I'd knock her ass out over Asylum with the quickness these days.

There was honestly nothing about my life that I would change at this point. My relationship with Sy was perfect, True was doing well, and our families and businesses were good. I didn't want to jinx it by saying things were perfect, but I was happy it seemed like life was finally back on its axis—lined up perfectly for Sy and I to do life together permanently.

The flight attendant hovered over us, asking, "Would you like water, orange juice, or champagne?" with a wide smile.

"We'll take champagne," Asylum replied.

"Actually... I need orange juice." Looking over at him, I confessed, "I won't be drinking alcohol for the next several months."

The flight attendant gasped and congratulated us, letting everyone in our section know I was pregnant. As they clapped and congratulated us, Asylum's head hung as he grinned. When he looked into my eyes, his were watery.

"I put a baby in you?" he confirmed, resting his hand on my stomach.

Chuckling, I teased him with, "Boy, as much as you were cumming in me, don't act like you surprised."

He laughed and pulled me closer for a kiss. "I love you," he muttered before kissing me again. "Thank you, sweetheart." He gave me another kiss. "I'm going to take care of you both, I promise." And another. "You won't have to want for anything. Thank you."

Asylum's forehead rested on mine as he thumbed my still flat belly. I kissed his cheeks then his lips, giggling at the goofy expression on his face. He pulled me close for another hug, and I was confident we'd probably spend this entire flight on each other's lips and in each other's arms.

Finally, after thirteen years, I was back with my asylum. My safe space. My protector. The man whose love had the ability to drive me crazy, yet somehow... filled me with peace and kept me sane.

THE END

AFTERWORD

Click:

To read Haley & Antonne's story.
To read Elite & Denali's story.

Merc is up next.

If you liked the thriller undertone Trey provided, preorder my first traditionally published thriller romance – *The Loyal Wife.*

Swipe for more information...

THE LOYAL WIFE

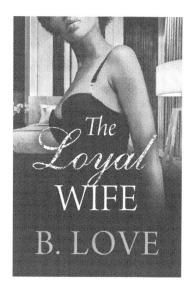

From Romance to Thriller...
B. Love makes her debut in traditional publishing with
"The Loyal Wife".
**An emotionally charged psychological thriller that will
leave fans breathless as they bear witness to the lengths**

a wife will go to honor her vows. An addictive page turner for fans of twisty plots in the same vein of Colleen Hoover's Verity.

Perfect wife... Perfect life... until you can't remember either.

The moment Dante Williams wakes up on the side of the road, unsure of where he is or who he is, his life changes for the worse. After a brief stay in the hospital, Dante is released to the care of his loving wife, Sade. Sade is beautiful, successful, and loyal. So loyal, she devotes herself to Dante indefinitely, hoping this will help him appreciate what he has—his life and his wife.

While seemingly having it all, their perfect marriage isn't enough to keep Dante from digging up the past in hopes of recovering his memory. It isn't long before he begins questioning Sade's behavior and intentions. Once secrets start to unravel, Dante is left more confused than the day following the accident.

When Dante discovers evidence of something more sinister at play, he prepares to end his marriage but learns quickly that Sade meant every word in her vows and plans to honor them, until death.

Releasing 2.20.2024 everywhere paperbacks are sold.
For a full list of retailers and to preorder, click here.

About the Author

Let's connect!

Mailing list - https://bit.ly/MLBLove22
On all social media - @authorblove
If you rave about this book on TikTok, tag me, and let's make a duet!
For exclusive eBooks, paperbacks, and audiobooks – www.prolificpenpusher.net

We hate errors, but we are human! If the B. Love team leaves any grammatical errors behind, do us a kindness and send them to us directly in an email to emailblove@gmail.com with ERRORS as the subject line.
As always, if you enjoyed this book, please leave a review on Amazon/Goodreads, recommend it on social media and/or to a friend, and mark it as READ on your Goodreads profile.

Follow B. on Amazon for updates on her releases by clicking here.

Made in the USA
Columbia, SC
02 July 2024

37876770R20111